GODS, GUNS, AND MONEY
ON THE
ROAD TO KEY WEST

D1496397

MICHAEL REISIG

eBook ISBN: 978-1-7363479-0-4
Paperback ISBN: 978-1-7363479-1-1

Cover design by Glassbrook Designs
Cover design copyright © 2019 Clear Creek Press

Published by Clear Creek Press
105 Dogwood Drive, Mena, AR 71953
1-479-394-4992

TO BEGIN THIS READ, let me offer a few words about the insightfulness of "lesser creatures," some of which you will find in this book. Having spent a lifetime with dogs, cats, and birds, I have come to realize that their intellect can be startling, and if you give them the latitude to become more than "just a possession," you are inevitably rewarded.

I have shared this life with a couple of extraordinary animals — one dog and one cat who absolutely pushed the envelope of primary intellect to a different level. And I had a raven whose memory just astounded me. I raised the bird from abandoned infancy for a short time. Its mother was killed protecting her nest and I found the flightless baby on the forest floor. I took care of it for a few weeks, feeding it with an eyedropper at first, then I gave it to the curator of a local wildlife center.

Several years later, I was visiting that same wildlife facility when a full-grown raven came swooping down out of the sky, calling excitedly. It landed squarely on my shoulder and rubbed itself against me. The curator of the facility shook his head in amazement as he stared at my confusion and surprise. "That's the same bird you gave me at your house, years ago," he said with a knowing grin. "He still hangs out here. That's the same damn bird..."

I will be forever grateful for the insight that my furred and feathered friends have given me.

— Michael Reisig

Acknowledgments

"I'm a really smart person and a wonderful writer, and I produced this entire book by myself."

If at any time you hear that from a genuinely successful novelist, you can be assured that you're dealing with a blind egotist or a pathological liar — or both.

I'll be the first to admit that without the help of a handful of extraordinarily talented people and a number of good friends who took the time to help fix a tale that was definitely fractured in places, you wouldn't be reading this now. I've been extremely fortunate to have incorporated many perceptive and clever folks, from editors and proofers and cover designers to numerous writer friends, in this and earlier endeavors. They have made my life, and my books, so much better.

First off, thanks to my primary beta reader, Virginia Williams, who always finds the initial battery of flaws. Then there's my first editor, Tim Slauter, whose remarkable insight cleaned and tightened this tale. In the midst of all this, there were a handful of my writer friends. A very special thanks to Nick Sullivan, Robert Simpson, David Thatcher Wilson, Don Rich, Wayne Stinnett, and John Cunningham.

Finally, of course, there is my incredibly talented primary editor, Cris Wanzer. She has, once again, taken what was collected and magically sculpted it into a professional, accurate medium for publishing. She's my "book magician."

Last but not least, there is my artistic cover designer, Sandra Glassbrook, who takes a handful of scribbled images and photos, and brings my covers to life.

Thank you all, my friends, so much.

Finally, this book is dedicated to veteran adventure novelist Ed Robinson, who passed away on November 22 of this year. He was greatly admired by all of us in the "adventure writing" community. He was a fine novelist and a fine man.

Sail on, Ed… Sail on…

CHAPTER ONE

Key West
Summer 1990

It was late July and hot enough to cook bacon on the sidewalk. Even the seagulls were seeking shade along the docks at Mallory Square. The bars were doing a bang-up business, and Crazy Eddie's was no exception. In Key West, there's no such thing as "happy hour," really. On this island, people start getting "happy" with their scrambled eggs and bacon, and they have a wide variety of "happy." Sip it, snort it, or pop it — no one judges, no one cares. This is the Sodom of the Caribbean, the Gomorrah of your wildest dreams — the island of delicious sins and remarkable sunsets. This is Key West.

It had been just about two months since our truly "incredible" Key West-Caribbean Race — a scavenger hunt beyond our wildest dreams. Hell, beyond *anyone's* wildest dreams. After that particularly challenging affair, neither Will nor I, or our immediate family (Jing, his daughter; and my son, Tax) had shown any inclination for a new adventure. It actually felt good to have no "contests" looming on the horizon.

Will and I had told the story of our latest adventure so many times we knew it virtually by rote, trading off in the recounting with a practiced cadence that seemed rehearsed. And, the most remarkable thing about a good tale is, it never gets less dynamic in the telling. Ask any adventurer.

We all sat around a table in the back. ("We" being most of the members of the Hole in the Coral Wall Gang.) Jing, in blue jeans and a loose Jimmy Buffett shirt, had even brought her huge osprey, Cielo, who perched in comfortable awareness on the back of a chair next to her — the creature's huge yellow eyes surveying all, missing nothing. Will called it "a damned Doberman with wings." Jing had raised it from a fledgling and there was a bond between them that fell somewhere between extraordinary and spooky. They were a remarkable pair — the blond-haired beauty and the purely dangerous gray-and-white sea hawk.

Her brother, Tax, sat quietly off to her left, enjoying a beer, watching the crowd and paying attention, much like the big hawk. He was dressed in cotton pants and a tight T-shirt that defined his trim physique. On occasion, he'd push back his long, sun-bleached hair, those hazel eyes sweeping the bar, ever the sentinel...

There was a most interesting story that went along with those two. Well over twenty years ago in the Keys, both Will and I were courting the same woman — the randy and beautiful Banyan McDaniel. In one of those nearly impossible situations (studied mostly in college biology), we both managed to impregnate her, resulting in non-identical twins. Long before anyone knew this had happened, she left us for a conga player in some sort of Caribbean Marimba band and disappeared into the sunset. Then, twenty years later, we ran into Tax and Jing at a bar in New Orleans. We were struck by how much they looked like us, and when we started trading histories, the lights came on. Shortly after that, we contacted their mother in Barbados and she confirmed it. While it was a mind-blowing situation, we soon discovered that we all felt a natural affinity for each other that developed into a family relationship. Damned strange but true... And that's how Will and I became midlife fathers.

Crazy Eddie, bar owner and senior member of the Hole in the Coral Wall Gang (who had lived up to his name more than once), had a waiter refresh our drinks. Eddie was a one-eyed, grizzled curmudgeon offset with a funky sense of humor and enough damned courage to rival Jeb Stuart at Bull Run. In addition, Eddie was our primary pilot, and he owned an older but well-maintained Grumman Goose floatplane that often served as our major source of transportation on various adventures.

Another old friend and member of "the club," Cody Joe, had also joined us. Cody, a graduate of ugly Southeast Asian jungles and nasty situations, and a connoisseur of good beer and fine women, resided on a handsome little forty-five-foot Morgan sailboat anchored in Key West Harbor. Our blond-haired, blue-eyed Casanova had just recently parted ways with his latest "yacht mate." (She was the most recent in a long conga line, and had lasted longer than most.) But the truth was, Cody was a free spirit — a very hard character to tie to a single cleat.

Arturio, our South American buddy and newest member of the gang, was back in Venezuela at the moment. Something to do with a knife fight over a woman at the Green Parrot. His attorney had recommended that he disappear for a while until some of the details could be "straightened out or paid off." Unfortunately, it sounded like this could be an extended situation.

The only other person missing from the gang was Travis Christian. Travis was possibly the apex of the team, and the leader, if you could say there was one. The six-foot-three, ex-Vietnam helicopter pilot powerhouse, with a "we're gonna do it my way" temperament was only just returning from a stay in England, where he had unsuccessfully pleaded with his longtime British girlfriend to come live with him in the Caribbean Islands. The long-distance relationship that had struggled for over a year appeared to have finally succumbed.

None of us were really looking for adventure at the time, but sometimes adventure has a way of finding you, whether you're looking for it or not. It's a bit of a long story, so grab yourself a beer…

We were sitting there, catching up, when Will picked up a copy of the *Key West Citizen*. He was paging through it and chuckled. "Animal Man has struck again," he muttered with a smile. He handed me the paper and there was a short article about someone torching a guy's car and taking his dog. The animal had been continuously tied to a pole outside a trailer, in the sun most of the time with little or no food or water. The neighbors had reported the owner to the authorities a couple of times, and the guy had received warnings from Animal Control, but each time he argued or threatened his way into keeping the dog.

I eased out an angry sigh. "You'd be amazed how difficult it is to take an animal away from an owner — even a bastard owner."

My friend paused and smiled, his blue eyes narrowing. "But it looks like Animal Man nailed the son of a bitch."

"Who's Animal Man?" I asked.

"It's an interesting story," my friend replied. "Apparently, there is somebody — a guy, I imagine...I suppose it's a guy — who watches out for animals that are being abused or mistreated in the Keys. If you know of someone who's mistreating an animal, you can leave a message on the pool table blackboard at Sloppy Joe's. There's a line scrawled at the bottom of the board. It says, *Do you know of a domestic creature, treated without mercy, punished without crime?"* Will smiled again. "Nobody erases that message or the replies, not even the bikers. You write a single line about the animal and an address. Then, it appears Animal Man does a reconnaissance. If he agrees with you, he does something about it."

"Like what?" I asked.

At that point, Eddie offered a humorless grin, instinctively adjusted his black eye patch, and leaned in on the table. "Actually, some pretty damned brutal shit, from what I hear through the grapevine. The serious offenders end up having vehicles 'accidentally' catch on fire, or they suffer from untimely muggings where nothing is taken." He exhaled, then continued. "One guy came home to find fifty pounds of dog shit distributed ingeniously throughout his home and all the water faucets on — with the drain stops in place. Another guy who was supposedly abusing horses out on Vaca Key found his fishing boat at the bottom of a canal — a half-dozen holes shot in the hull. *A.M.* was spray-painted on the side."

Will eased out a breath. "Some people get worse reminders regarding their bad manners. A couple of people claim to have awakened at night to find a man standing over their bed wearing a Halloween-type dog mask and carrying an electric cattle prod. For them, it was an experience they won't soon forget."

"What do the police think about this?" I asked.

My buddy shrugged again. "Well, it's not that they're not investigating. Some of this shit adds up to serious property damage...and assault, at the least." Then he shrugged and smiled. "But the damned truth is, the guy is becoming sort of a cult hero in the Lower Keys, and it appears more animals are being treated better now because the owners are scared shitless that they might get a visit from Animal Man."

I laughed out loud, shaking back my shoulder-length hair. "That is just too freaking cool!"

Will shrugged. "Well, at first I think he just went around looking, you know? But now, he's getting a reputation. People started using that blackboard at Sloppy Joe's. Don't know how that started for sure, but that's the program now."

"What a damned cool guy," I whispered in admiration. "Somebody doing something about bad things. You gotta admire him…"

My friend offered a knowing grin. "Yeah, no one should be afraid to be an Animal Man."

Cody offered a feral smile. "A man after my own heart. I wonder if he needs any help. I could get into that…you know, as a hobby."

Will shook his head and smiled. "I don't think so, buddy. Knowing you, the offenders would soon be missing appendages — ears and fingers — just to remind them of their transgressions. Animal Man seems to have found just the right combination of righteousness and retribution, and right now, he's got the community on his side.

"So…" said Tax, leaning in toward the table a little and glancing around at us. "When are we heading out on another adventure?"

"Jesus!" muttered Eddie. "You just got back from a freakin' harrowing gig, dude! Maybe you don't remember the freakin' giant lizards or being chased by Haitian voodooers, or your sailboat sinking, and you being bound to a channel marker for three days, during which time we all thought you were dead. How about you catch your breath here a little?"

There were chuckles around the table.

"Youth has a short memory," mumbled Cody. He glanced at Tax. "Give us a chance to discover another windmill, Don Q." But Cody paused then and shrugged. "Although I have been getting a little bored lately." He smiled. "And I'm sort of between 'company' at the moment."

"Well, you know," said Jing tentatively. "There is another windmill… There's the possibility of the crystal skulls in Venezuela." She turned to me. "That was a fantastic story you came home with — the old shaman and the tale of an ancient crystal skull or two that might have survived the ravages of man and time. That perhaps came from someplace far, far away…" She looked around at the others, then fixed those incredible blue eyes on me again. "You yourself said you might have seen a cave when you were parachuting down off the cliff in that Texan's crazy Venezuelan contest — a face in the rocks and 'a mote in God's eye' you called it, that fit the description the old shaman had given you." She offered that beguiling smile. "Wouldn't that be a find? If a genuine ancient crystal skull could be located and verified as being tooled outside our common, modern practices? Something that perhaps possesses qualities beyond our immediate understanding?"

Jing tossed back her blond mane, turning on the charm. But I wasn't fooled and I wasn't succumbing.

"And it's nice and simple — nothing really complicated," she added, as if she didn't care that much. "We just locate the spot and simply rappel down the wall to check it out." She held out her hands, palms up, and shrugged. "Bing, bam, boom…"

"Where have I heard that before?" I muttered. *"It's nice and simple…"* I wagged a forefinger. "There ain't no such thing as nice and simple in the adventuring business. And that glimpse I caught of that cave opening — if that's what it was — was brief at best." I paused, then spoke, mostly to myself. "I'll admit that there was some consistency to the old shaman's story there. I did see what sort of appeared like eyes and a narrow mouth in the wall. But I'm not about to —"

Tax looked over and held up a hand. "We all know it's a bit of a long shot, Dad. It's okay. We don't need to make any decisions about another wild trip right away."

I eased out a breath and glanced at Will. He exhaled gratefully.

"We can wait a week or so," continued Tax. "Let you old guys catch your breath."

Damn, that boy knew how to wound you softly…

CHAPTER TWO

About that same time, a few miles away on Stock Island, Rinco Rodriguez (AKA "Animal Man") was doing a preliminary reconnoiter on a target — a dog that had been tied to a tree for three days with some water and not much in the way of food. He was about to fix that. Rodriguez was very good at the "reconnoiter business." The U.S. Marines had trained him well before they sent him into Iraq. He did a lot of reconnoitering there, in hellholes called Fallujah and Baghdad. And he got good at it. It was what kept him alive. It was why he came home when others didn't...

Well, that wasn't the only reason he came home in one piece. He worked with a dog there in Concealed Ordinance Location and Identification and he came to admire — actually, love — that dog very much. He wasn't ashamed of it at all. That damned animal, Custer, was incredible, and he had saved Captain Rodriguez's life more than once. In the end, only two weeks before they were coming home, Custer gave his life for his human companion when he spotted a partially buried mine that Rinco had missed. The dog literally threw himself at the captain, knocking him down and away as the wire was tripped and the small anti-personnel bomb exploded.

Custer was given a burial with honors but it mattered little to Captain Rodriguez. He had lost his best friend. A month later, when his tour was over, they sent him home, and when his time was up, he didn't re-enlist. He packed up what few belongings he had and moved to the green sea and sunshine of Key West. He wanted to forget the pain he'd seen and just lie in the sun for a while. But oddly enough, he discovered another battle — an injustice if you will. It started when he watched his neighbor tie his dog in the sun when he went to work, and feed him only when he remembered, and beat the poor animal anytime it pleased him.

One day, Rinco's neighbor was taking a stick to the tied animal because it had the audacity to defecate near the steps of the trailer, where he was tied. The captain snapped. The neighbor ended up in the hospital and the dog ended up with Rodriguez, and somehow, Animal Man was born.

By the end of the evening at Crazy Eddie's Bar and Swill, we were all comfortably buzzed. We'd told a few stories (that everyone had heard before), we were flush with the comfort of liquor and friends, and we were content with the possibility that maybe, just maybe, another adventure might yet be waiting around the corner. But no one was in a hurry. Well, maybe that's not true. Tax and Jing would have left the following morning had it been an option.

The truth was, I was a little more intrigued by this concept than I let on. Long story short, I remembered quite clearly what the old shaman in the Venezuelan village had said to Will and me only a few weeks ago, as we tried to escape his psychopathic son and make it to the cliffs and the sea for the parachuting contest we were supposed to be participating in.

I had always been fascinated by the possibility of life on other planets, and I was more than intrigued by the early civilizations like the Mayans, the Incas, and the Egyptians, who we now knew were far more advanced than was originally accepted. (With all our advancements, we have difficulty rivaling their incredible architecture today, and in particular, their pyramids.) And there were the fabled Atlanteans as well, whose apparent ruins we were only just discovering in the Atlantic and Mediterranean seas. I remembered the old shaman's words quite clearly…

"A thousand moons ago, it was said there was a strange race that would appear, sometimes in flying houses, to offer suggestions for the timing of planting crops, strange healing concepts, metallurgy, and the nature of the stars. They made it clear that, in their absence, the crystal skulls could be a reminder of the breadth of a god's knowledge."

I remembered how the little shaman's eyes had grown distant and he exhaled heavily. "But that was a long time ago, and those who lived here then eventually forgot their lessons…" He sighed again. "We still fought, we still stole, and we still lied for gain. Sadly, very few of the crystal skulls survived our carnage, and gradually, our communes with a distant enlightenment waned."

I was lost in that extraordinary history lesson, as fantastic as it was.

"Eventually, the visits of the star voyagers ended," the old shaman said with a weary shrug. "I think they gave up on us. Nonetheless, a few of the crystal skulls had faithfully been passed on from shaman to shaman." He paused and spit into the fire. It hissed in anger. "Unfortunately, the world our people had known was changing. We found ourselves fighting for survival against a host of angry god-like bearded men in giant canoes, who came from the other side of the sky." He drew in a sharp breath. "At first, we thought these new invaders might be the gods who had assisted us so greatly in the past." The old fellow slapped the earth angrily. "It was a colossal mistake! These new 'gods' in shiny metal clothes brought disease, greed, and death, and the result was the destruction of our societies. They gradually took everything of value, from our women and our religion to our way of life. But before all was lost, there was a gathering of leaders in the region. It was decided that the last remaining crystal skull we possessed was to be hidden, beyond the reach of these new monsters."

Now all this, of course, had caught Will and me immediately. Will, ever the historian, was really taken. But the last part was the best.

"A council of our chiefs and shamans took place in the valley below us," continued the shaman, his eyes partially closed now, his head bobbing slightly as he spoke. "It was decided that somewhere in the great, inaccessible cliffs that greeted the ocean, would be the resting place for our last gift from the sky people. The bravest of our warriors were sent on a quest, searching for a suitable haven for the last crystal skull, and there it would rest until the gods saw fit to visit us again." The shaman paused once more, drew a shaky breath, and gazed out in the direction of the coast. "It is said that the skull became a mote in the left eye of a mournful face in a distant cliff that faced the great water. To rest until the gods called again. That is the legend..."

It was all just surreal. There was a possibility that we were talking about a device that possibly allowed some sort of telepathic communication. Maybe... And maybe it was just a crystal skull. The ultimate sadness in all this was, the people who knew about this remarkable connection had been destroyed in a massive, mindless genocide conducted by European conquistadores. The first people the Spanish killed were the priests, who possessed all the old knowledge, then they destroyed their written words in bonfires of righteous idiocy. They had learned early on that if you can kill a man's faith, you can destroy him.

I had asked the old shaman one final question. "Why a skull ... and not a face? I mean, a skull is not exactly beguiling — it doesn't lend a sense of comfort."

The ancient shaman raised his head to look at me. He held up a scrawny forefinger. "Because a skull says, 'this is who I am, underneath...with all de guise stripped away.' A face can be pretty when the spirit is not. A face can lie."

He was right. A skull contains the nexus of intellect and conscience.

I recalled that Will, the self-ordained historian for the Hole in the Coral Wall Gang, had reined me in and slapped me with reality.

"But all this freaks out most conventional faiths, and the mainstream archaeological and scientific communities aren't buying much of this either. It would mean that there was a lot more going on around this planet, in this universe, a lot earlier than we've been required to believe. While we've obviously had some fake crystal skulls appear here and there, many people believe that at least a few of these unique relics can't be explained away as hot air balloons, and may have actually been the products of extraordinary civilizations, such as the Mayans or the Egyptians, or perhaps something or someone outside this green-and-blue ball we live on."

Will exhaled bitterly. "That damned bunch of Smithsonian sociopaths always seems to be leading the charge in refuting anything counter-conventional. They want science and religion firmly in their grasp, and they don't like change. I told you a while back that the Smithsonian's recent electron microscope analyses on some eighteenth-century crystal skull finds in Central America said the markings on the skulls could only have been made with modern carving implements. So they can't be genuine antiquities." He shook his head. "Skulls with modern-style tool processing actually credit the concept that they could have been made by advanced civilizations centuries ago! And just because a skull was *found* in the 1800s doesn't necessarily mean it was *made* in the 1800s, or that it was made where it was found." My friend sighed heavily and offered an almost sad smile. "He who crushes imagination destroys the future."

I was reminded of the words of the little Venezuelan bandito, Torro, who said, "Sonwhere out dere is a hole in a mountain wall where dat shiny head is hidden. Da man who find dat can talk to da gods… If dey still got da same number…"

I doubted that was true, exactly…but I found myself getting that old heat again and that pronounced itch for the unknown.

It could be we were "booking a new gig," as Crazy Eddie would say.

The following morning, I met Will for breakfast on Summerland Key. It was a short drive for both of us — him up from Key West and me down from Big Pine Key. I realized we needed to talk a little before we committed ourselves, and our offspring, to another adventure.

"So what do you think, *amigo?*" I asked over coffee. "Is this wild goose chase really worth the effort? I mean, this is all about a look into a cave — if we can find the cave — in the side of a cliff. If it's actually a cave…"

"It's also about some serious freaking dangling and rappelling," Will added cautiously.

I nodded. "Yeah, you're right. The hole in that cliff, if it's there, is probably a hundred feet down from the top. You've got winds to contend with, uneven terrain, and God knows what else." I eased out a sigh. "I'll tell you the truth. If this wasn't such a freaking fascinating thing — if I hadn't seen the light of almost religious conviction in the eyes of that old shaman — I wouldn't be remotely interested in this."

Will shrugged. "I gotta admit, it's not like we need the money or we're anxious for the notoriety." He sighed. Then he offered that half-grin of his. "It's really more like a family outing thing. Some families go on picnics at the lake or go fishing on Sunday after church. We fly across hundreds of miles of treacherous ocean, to a place known for bandits and Indians, so we can scale down the side of a treacherous cliff to possibly locate an ancient artifact that we have about a one-in-a-hundred chance of finding."

I returned his smile. "Yeah, we're not exactly *Family Circle* parents. But what the hell? It is what it is. You only go around once at a time. So go for the gusto. Besides, it's challenges like this that add dimension to your life. I wouldn't deny the kids that. We might actually be able to offer our offspring some tangible proof that we are only one small part of the fabric of intelligent life in the universe. That's a huge thing. That makes this worthwhile."

Will nodded sagely. "I've said it before — scientists are estimating there are billions of solar systems in our galaxy alone. *Billions*. It defies logic and intellect to think that in a panorama that vast, there are no other intelligent creatures to be found." My friend paused and drew a breath. "As much as I love my conventional faith in God, I'm also forced to recognize the possibility that we are not the only clay He shaped, and Earth may not be the only place He had a potter's wheel."

My friend did a smooth one-eighty and turned to me. "But here's the thing. I think we need to reduce the danger in this whole affair by incorporating Crazy Eddie and his big Grumman Goose. With its long-range tanks, it's got the fuel capacity to jump the southern pond without sweating. And it's an amphibian as well." He smiled. "Eddie's been sitting behind that bar for too long. He'll leap at a little adventure. And I wouldn't be at all surprised to see Cody and Travis join us, just for some 'recreation.' That would make for a pretty safe gig with the kids."

"You've already thought this out and packaged it," I said with a grin.

Will nodded. "Yep. Yep, I have. A nice, relatively safe, family outing to South America."

"Like an Easter egg hunt...for ancient skulls."

My friend smiled. "Yeah, exactly..."

CHAPTER THREE

Crazy Eddie didn't even hesitate. "So, when do we leave?" he said after my brief explanation. He was definitely a man in need of adventurous relief.

Ironically enough, the idea appealed to Cody and Travis as well. Travis had just come in the night before, after a long series of flights from England. Cody was ready to head out the door but Travis needed a couple of days to get his stateside affairs in order. Nonetheless, a little adventure sounded like the ticket for relief from his mangled love affair. They agreed to fly out a day or two behind us in Cody's long-range Turbo Cessna 310 so we gave them the coordinates for the area. Both aircraft would first clear Customs in Caracas, Venezuela, then fly to the cliffs where we had participated in the big Texan promoter's parachuting contest, just west of Caracas. Brazos Bonham had bulldozed a strip on the ridge near the cliffs so the contestants could get their aircraft in and out. It had only been about a month ago but it seemed like ages. (There were times in my life when I wished I were a writer. I thought the whole affair — the contest, with all the crazy characters — would have made a great novel.)

Tax and Jing were ecstatic. Both agreed that they could be packed and ready in an hour.

"Whoa! Hold on," said Will, holding up his hands with a smile. "We've got things to get together. You need to pack a bag each for about a week. I don't see us down there for any longer than that. Either there's a cave or there isn't, and this is not an Easter egg hunt. If we don't find what we're looking for after a couple of days, we're headed home. And you can't bring weapons — they're too damned much trouble with Customs down there. But you can tuck away a stun gun and a knife of your choice."

No one could dampen the kids' enthusiasm. As Tax put it, "We're coming home with a freaking skull that's gonna drop the collective jaws at the Smithsonian."

"I'm not all that anxious to tell the Smithsonian squat," muttered Will. "Have you forgotten how they reacted the last time

13

we embarrassed them — with the Egyptian artifacts in the Grand Canyon?"

He made a good point. The room got quiet for a moment.

Speaking of the Smithsonian...

Richard Thomason was shuffling papers on his desk when one of his "investigative operatives" knocked and entered his office. Thomason sat down the papers, combed his dark hair back with the fingers of one hand, and looked up, his gray eyes indifferent. He was the new director of the organization and had replaced Professor Aaron Baal, who had apparently decided to jump off of his eleventh-story balcony in Washington, D.C. a few months earlier.

"What can I do for you, Briggs?"

Briggs, a big fellow with blond hair, green eyes, and the square jaw of a boxer, exhaled slightly. "I got a little slice of information from one of our people in the Florida Keys. I thought I might pass it on. You remember that group of people who were involved in the Grand Canyon incident — the discovery of the ancient city there?"

"Yeah, yeah, I remember," Thomason replied cautiously. No one wanted any credit for that fiasco. "That was before my present position, but I remember..."

"Looks like that same group of people — the folks from Key West — are preparing to chase something else. I thought it might be of interest to you."

Thomason cocked his head. "Okay, you have my attention."

"Word on the street is they're preparing for a gig of some sort in Venezuela. One of our people down there heard a conversation involving a guy who owns a bar there. Evidently, they're chasing a rumor regarding a couple of the fabled ancient crystal skulls of South and Central America."

Thomason eased out a breath and smiled grimly. "We keep putting out that fire and it just keeps flaming up somewhere else. Nothing to it. Just a legend, that's all. People keep claiming to have found something significant but it always turns out to be smoke. Replications, and mostly poor ones at that."

Briggs drew back a little and his brow furrowed. "But I

understand we have a couple..." He paused. "...that we've taken from discoveries..."

Thomason waved him off. "Just a precaution on our part. Nothing that could be actually verified." He paused as if he'd had second thoughts. "But...these folks have caused the Smithsonian some...*difficulty*...in the past. Just for the hell of it, why don't you call Miami and have them put a small team on it? Just so we know what's going on..."

When Briggs had gone, the Smithsonian director eased out a hard breath and slid back his chair. The truth was, the last affair with those people from the Keys had turned into a serious fiasco. The Smithsonian lost a director and several "agents," and was denied a major archaeological find. He wasn't anxious to repeat anything like that. And actually, the skulls in question here weren't all exactly smoke and mirrors. The Smithsonian had one in the special storage room they called "the basement" that just...spooked him. There was something about it — the antiquity for sure, and the extraordinary workmanship, requiring tooling processes that challenged anything the modern world had. But there was "a feeling" that emanated from it — an understanding. It was like the damned thing could reach inside his head. It scared him. And he was not a person who ruffled easily.

Thomason exhaled. No, the world was not ready for some things — things that could change intellects and concepts, and perhaps history. And that was not a good thing. No need to confuse the masses — altering perceptions that were welded into place by covenants with religion, politics, and history. He shook his head, staring ahead sightlessly. *No, not a good idea at all...*

By the end of the week, everything was pretty much in order and we were ready to go. Travis and Cody would follow in their 310 in two days. Will and I, along with Tax and Jing, would fly over in Eddie's Grumman Goose. This time, I decided to bring Shadow. That dog had a second sense about people and situations that I thoroughly appreciated. And while this seemed like an easy enough gig, I liked the idea of having the hearing and perception that animal possessed.

Jing, of course, was bringing Cielo, her osprey. I had seen that creature earn his keep enough times for me to welcome its presence. Ironically enough, Shadow had taken a liking to Jing's hawk. How or why I don't really know, but Cielo seemed to be quite comfortable with the arrangement as well. I started noticing that when we were all gathered together, Shadow would end up settling in somewhere near Cielo. Even more amazing was the hawk's reaction. He intuitively seemed to recognize this "affection," if that's what it could be called, and in his own austere way, seemed to appreciate it.

We had packed minimal supplies — mostly MRE-type meals, and a bag or two of fruit and high-energy candy bars. This was going to be a short gig. It wouldn't take long in this somewhat esoteric voyage to know if the dam held water.

Eddie had filed a flight plan that would take us along the northwestern coast of Cuba and into Port-au-Prince, Haiti, where we would refuel his long-range tanks. From there, we'd "shoot the pond" (fly across the open sea between Cuba and South America) into Caracas, Venezuela, where we'd clear Customs. From there it was only a half-hour flight to the little strip near the cliffs between Machurucuto and Boca de Uchire. My only worry was that the strip was a little small — hastily bulldozed for a few small twin engines.

Eddie asked me if the strip ended at the edge of the cliffs pointing out at the sea. I said yes. He just laughed and waved me off. "Then we'll just run off the cliff," he said with a smile. "We got fifteen hundred feet before we hit the sea. The old girl will catch the wind by then, I figure…"

Will just shook his head nervously. "Some things never change," he muttered. "Sonabitch thinks he's bulletproof. Or crash-proof."

I had to grin. "For all the wrecked airplanes he's walked away from, maybe he is."

It all started out just fine. It was a beautiful day — lots of sunshine, just a touch of wind. It looked like the gods were going to be kind to us. But I was reminded of an expression by our old Jamaican Rastaman buddy, Rufus. *"Never trust da gods, mon. You*

nothin' but live entertainment to dem, and dey make da rules."
He was right…

The flight around Cuba and into Port-au-Prince was uneventful, although the weather people mentioned that it looked like there was a disturbance building in the southern Caribbean. We hoped to push down and into Venezuela before it became an issue. Eddie didn't seem to be worried, so I let it ride, but I did take the copilot's seat. My older friend looked over at me and nodded his approval. He seemed unperturbed but I should have remembered that Eddie hardly worried about squat, and sometimes that philosophy bit him on the ass.

We were about seventy-five miles out of Caracas and the sun was just lingering above the horizon when the southeastern sky started darkening. Inside another fifteen minutes, the horizon in front of us had begun blackening. Caracas weather was now reporting a band of severe thunderstorms with powerful, near-hurricane winds sweeping eastward along the coast of Venezuela, from Maracaibo to Vera Cruz, with the possibility of embedded tornadoes.

"Hmm…" mumbled Eddie as everyone gathered around the cockpit. "Looks like it's gonna get a little sticky." He checked his radar again, then turned to us. "There ain't no getting around this son of a bitch." Our pilot exhaled heavily. "We're a little close on fuel and we can't afford to outrun it or turn around, and the freakin' seas are too rough to just land in open water, so we're just gonna damn the torpedoes and take it in. Maybe we can beat this muther before the worst hits."

Our grizzled pilot/friend was always an optimist.

Fifteen minutes later, things were deteriorating rapidly. The storm was pushing us well east of Caracas now. The good news was, that was closer to our actual destination (just east of Rio Chico), and I was getting glimpses of the coast in the distance through the rain. But right now, just flying this aircraft was becoming a challenge. Lightning was stabbing the darkening sky everywhere you looked, and we were being rocked like a Wild Mouse carnival ride. Eddie's normally easy, confident demeanor was fading to beaded sweat and serious concern. The lines in his face had tightened into crevices, and his one eye had lost that typical bold confidence.

(Only those of you who have piloted a plane or a boat into the jaws of a truly ugly meteorological disturbance really understand this feeling of being disconnected from human reprieve, of realizing you are no longer in control. It's a damned scary thing when luck and chance are the only friends you have left. Those of you who have been there are nodding now...)

We had reached the Venezuelan coast, but we had been pushed well east. I had no idea where. The sun had found its way into the horizon and everything was dark gray. Eddie and I were flying blind, dropping down, trying to find a way out of the worst of it, when all of a sudden there was a brilliant, hammering explosion off the port wing. Amid the cries and yells, Eddie glanced out of his window as the aircraft slowly started to roll over. He and I were already instinctively reducing power on the port engine and augmenting control with the rudder and ailerons to bring us back to straight and level. As best we could, anyway.

"Lightning got us!" my old friend yelled, fighting the controls. "Looks like the electrical shock damaged the port engine as well, but freaking worse, that aileron looks like it's been bent and locked down. If I let go of the stick, she wants to roll over!"

Just to show me, he eased up on his control and the Goose started to roll. I cried out a little just then, I'll admit, as the realization came in a savage burst. If we didn't keep continuous control on the stick, the old girl was going to drop into a spinning dive and bury herself — and us — in the mountains below.

Just then, as if things couldn't get worse, the starboard engine coughed. It didn't quit, but it coughed. If that one quit, we'd be going down in a mountainous jungle, in a storm, with no power. That was a sure-fire recipe for visiting dead relatives.

Eddie salvaged the power but the engine spit and shuddered. "I'm thinking bad fuel," he grumbled as he pushed the throttle in and out a bit in an attempt to keep the fuel flowing. "Never buy fuel from a Haitian who's snorting cocaine when he thinks you're not watching," he added, referencing our recent fueling stop back in Port-au-Prince.

A flash of lightning burst off the port wing and brought us all back to the immediate problem. Eddie glanced around, then growled harshly, "This old girl ain't gonna make it to a strip. Hell, at this point we've been pulled off course enough that I don't even know where a landing field is."

Once more, our only engine shuddered and Eddie fought with the controls to keep us straight and level.

"If I let go of this stick, we're gonna roll over and fall like a dead pigeon," our pilot said. "And there ain't no such thing as a good crash landing in a mountainous jungle…in a freaking storm."

Eddie pulled up the nose a little, then came back to us. There was an odd look in his eye. I didn't like it…

"Here's what it comes down to," he said. There was a pause. "And I'm okay with it."

But I could see the fear and regret on his face.

"There are four parachutes in the back. You know where they are. I showed you yesterday when we were loading. You folks put them on, grab your animal friends, and jump. I'll get off a mayday now, with a position, so they'll be looking for you by morning."

At that moment, lightning struck again off the starboard wing, as if to emphasize the situation. The plane lurched and Eddie barely managed to bring us back to straight-and-level flight.

"Eddie, we can't do this," I whispered. "I just can't —"

"Shut up!" my old friend barked. "You're wasting valuable time. We're over the coast now. You need to jump before you get into the heavy jungle."

Will started to argue. "We can't leave you! Maybe we can rig the controls —"

In answer, Eddie looked at him and took his hands off the trembling yoke. The plane immediately lurched over toward the port side and started to fall. Everyone screamed. Eddie quickly brought it back before it became something that would cost him control.

He looked up at us again. "Get your chutes on, get your animals, and get the door open…" But at that moment he sighed and his eyes softened with acceptance. "And get the hell out of here," he said. "Go…live…dudes…"

And so, with regret that burned holes in our stomachs, we did. We silently gathered our animals. At the last moment, Jing slipped off the hood on her hawk's head, whispering to him the whole time in that strange language they shared and pulling him into her breast. The girl knew there was a chance she wouldn't survive the drop, and if she was...gone...a hood on the bird would be a death sentence.

I opened the custom sliding door, and as the wind ripped at us, we held each other silently for a moment. There were no good words for this. Then Jing went into her dad's arms for an emotional embrace. Then she pulled back and whispered, *"Vaya con Dios,"* turned, and jumped out into the howling darkness.

My son and I stared at each other for an emotionally charged moment, then he came into my arms. He had tears in his eyes but he wasn't afraid. He was a man now, and I loved what I saw. With one last touch of his cheek, I pulled away and he offered that beautiful, brave smile of his, then turned and stepped out into the darkness and was swept away.

I swung around to Will, and he was staring at me with a look somewhere between sadness and pride. "I'll see you later," he whispered. "No matter what..."

"You know the place," I said over the wind.

"Yeah," he replied with a smile. "The bar on the beach, with the jukebox." Then he jumped.

I grabbed Shadow and pulled him up against my chest, throwing his paws over my shoulders and drawing him into me like a lover. Then I took one last look at the cockpit. Eddie had turned and was watching. Our eyes met and he offered a small, two-finger salute. With that, he returned to his instruments. I clutched Shadow tightly and without another word, jumped out into the howling darkness after Will, "taking it to the limit" one more time.

As I fell, I watched my family disappear into the darkness. I saw Jing release her hawk as she fell away into the clawing wind. The bird's best chance in this was to be free and Jing knew it.

The wind tore at me with tiny, evil fingers as I tumbled at first, taking a moment to get my balance in the fall. I could see Will's chute blossoming a few hundred yards below me. Carefully, while holding Shadow in a death grip with one arm, I reached up and pulled my chute cord. Instantly, I felt that familiar pop and rush of silk, and a second later, there was the reassuring snap of the chute opening and catching air. But I almost lost Shadow when the chute opened. I screamed, digging my fingers into his thick fur and pulling him against me. But the pop of the parachute had cost me my grip on the dog. He was no small creature, weighing in at about a hundred and ten pounds, and he had slipped slightly down around my waist. With the howling wind and being hammered about by the storm, he was gradually shifting toward my hips.

We were sailing down rapidly. At the same time, I could still see Will's chute just a few hundred yards south of me. Thanks to a full moon breaking through the clouds occasionally, I could also see the shadows of the jungle below. I was trying to stay in sight of my partner, but suddenly, a gust of wind struck me and jerked me nearly vertically. With absolute terror, I realized I was losing my grip on Shadow. He was simply too heavy and we were being slammed about by the fierce winds. I had dug my fingers into his fur like claws. I knew I was hurting him. I could hear him whining in pain. But he knew. He understood I was trying to save him, and he was clinging as best he could to my hips and legs. I grabbed his collar, trying desperately to hold him, but his weight was too great and the latch broke.

I found myself screaming in frustration as my boy began to slip away. He had no chance of survival in a fall. We were still a couple hundred feet above the jungle. I can't remember ever being more filled with terror. I was losing my companion, my friend, and there was nothing I could do. At the last moment, I saw a river just a few hundred yards to the west. With one hand, I pulled the maneuvering lines like a madman, aiming for it while my other hand clutched Shadow.

I wasn't quite there when I finally lost my grip. I remember looking down and seeing his terrified eyes, and crying out as I watched him fall away from me. *I still remember it sometimes, when I'm trying to sleep at night. He was frightened, petrified, but for just a moment, as my grip failed and I screamed into the night wind, I swear those eyes held with an understanding and the final gift of love. I have to believe it. It's all I have sometimes…*

Cielo tumbled more than flew across the dark, lightning-filled sky. The near-hurricane winds ripped at him, and more than once the frightened creature lost control, plummeting downward in a barely controlled plunge. Instinct told him he needed to be on the ground, or in a low, protected tree somewhere. By the time he had fought his way to the safety of the jungle and a huge, fire-hollowed tree, he was miles and miles from his starting point. Cielo was battered, exhausted, and lost. He pulled himself farther into the crevice of the tree, shook like a dog, and hissed angrily.

The hawk had no idea that his lady and her brother had been caught in an aberrant updraft spawned by a small tornado. It had sucked them up and away, like something out of a *Wizard of Oz* tale, and carried them nearly twenty miles northeast. But sadly, that was not the worst of it...

They tell me, *"The calamity you remember on occasion is not as bad as the one you can't forget."* I understand that now.

I didn't know it at the time, but my old friend, Eddie, had forced all he could from his aging, storm-damaged Goose. By the time all his friends had parachuted out, there was little control left. The starboard engine had long since died and he was fighting gravity and Mother Nature with a sputtering, coughing port engine that had no interest in survival. A moment later, it too gave up the ghost and Eddie found himself headed down into an unforgiving jungle with nearly no control of his airplane.

Then the jungle came surging up at him with ugly indifference. The plane tore into the shadowy darkness of bough and vine, and the old girl moaned as she was ripped apart. Eddie was torn from his seat and thrown forward against the yoke and the panel. He felt his ribs crack as the starboard wing ripped itself free and spun away violently. The plane turned on its side and the remaining wing jerked upward as the aircraft gouged a flaming, hundred-yard furrow in the dark foliage. The old pilot was hurled across the cockpit like a ragdoll and slammed against a window, which smashed into vicious shards. His head hammered against an interior frame. Then it stopped...and everything, the entire jungle, went quiet. The last thing the old pilot noticed was how quiet it was. He closed his eye for just a few seconds...

A few moments later, when the creatures around the shattered aircraft had just begun to breathe again, the battered hull hissed violently as the flames found the fractured main gas tanks, and the remains exploded into a fiery ball.

Shadow and I had made it just far enough along in the lightning-filled sky to give my friend a chance at life. Just as I lost him, we were hit by a horrendous gust of wind, and given the short distance to the river, it was just enough to force him over the water below. I watched as he tumbled blindly through the air, then into the swelling, rolling tributary. Then he was gone.

Shadow's breath was knocked from him when he hit the water, and for a moment he lost consciousness, but the choking water brought him back and he managed to get his head above the surface. He was a "Keys dog" who loved the ocean and our canal behind the house, and swam better than most people I knew.

For the next twenty minutes, he was carried downstream, into the mountain heartland of Venezuela. Finally, he fought his way to the shoreline and managed to drag himself onto the trunk of an old tree that had fallen into the water, then to dry land. Well, *drier* land… Shadow lay there gasping, heaving, partway up a bank, not ten feet from the rapids. It was as far away as the last of his energy would take him.

It turned out to be enough.

CHAPTER FOUR

There was, of course, no way of knowing what happened to my companions. Given our intermittent jumps, we were probably spread out over five or ten miles. The only one I got to watch for a while was Will as we seemed to be drifting in a similar direction. But all I could do now was concentrate on trying to get down alive, given the vicious winds and the thick jungle below. Surviving the fall was only half the package. Beneath me was the river, and a heavy, rain-splashed canopy of green and brown, and night had arrived. There was no controlling much and I didn't have any idea where to land, so I just rolled with Mother Nature's punches, soaring haphazardly as I plummeted into the dark, verdant landscape below. As I finally reached the jungle itself, I caught one last glimpse of Will's battered parachute to the west, fluttering desperately to keep enough wind for a moment, then sailing into a rolling landscape of larger trees.

I recall thinking I had been pretty lucky so far, when a gust of wind hit me, slamming me down to just a few feet above the ground, and a huge rubber tree trunk suddenly materialized out of the mist. That was the last thing I remembered. Really, the last thing I remembered...

Shakespeare once said, *"There are more things in heaven and earth, Horatio, than are dreamt of in your philosophy."* I agree now.

When I hit the tree, in my very last moments of consciousness, I knew I was badly hurt. Then it all went black. But it didn't end there. Suddenly, there was a "whoosh" and was being drawn along in a huge, whirling tunnel. It seemed I had barely closed my eyes when I found myself sitting in the sand outside a lovely little thatched-roof island bar. The beach off to the side was picture-perfect and I could hear the gentle waves lapping at the shore. The sun was wonderful and warm. I could hear the melody of one of my favorite '70s songs in the wind — "California Dreaming."

It was just extraordinary...beyond anything I had ever experienced. I looked over at the shack and thought I could see someone sitting at the bar — tall and lanky, his blond hair down to his shoulders, his usual tropical tan, and his blue eyes focused out at the water. He turned to me then and smiled. *My buddy, Will!*

Everything seemed so perfect…like I never wanted to leave this spot. But then a girl appeared and walked over to me. She was calm and beautiful, and barefoot, with long blond hair, and she was wearing a tight-fitting blue sarong.

It was just so wonderful, I thought I'd died and gone to Heaven…

But then the girl looked at me and somewhat sadly shook her head. "I'm sorry," she said, "but you can't stay." She tilted her head slightly and offered an enigmatic smile. "It's not your time…"

Then it all melted with another "whoosh" and I found myself back on the hard jungle floor, with blood running down the side of my head and rain slapping my face. Gradually, with a moan, I managed to work myself to a sitting position. That was the good news. The bad news was immediately forthcoming. I looked around and down at myself, and paused to try a little recall — and suddenly discovered that my mental well was…dry. I paused, drew a breath and shook my head, looked down at my clothes, and tried again — and got the same result. I had absolutely no idea who I was, or what I was, or where I came from. All I knew for sure was my head hurt like hell, and I was way too damned dizzy to stand. I just sat there, in the wet jungle, staring upward, lost to heaven, and apparently welcomed to hell. I tried again at recall. Nothing. Zip. I closed my eyes and softly slipped away, thinking maybe I could find my way back to that bar on the beach…

The good news was, it appeared I'd had a glimpse of "the other side"…maybe. And I was still alive. Evidently, they had thrown me out. It wasn't the first time I'd been thrown out of a bar. The bad news was, I saw someone over there. *My friend…*I thought. *My friend?*

The rain continued to hammer me as the night passed. The inclement weather finally surrendered and the sun gradually fought its way through a hazy, gray sky, then set once more. Sometime later, I had no idea exactly when, I awoke and found myself in a small but comfortable bed in a bamboo hut with mud-plastered, whitewashed walls and what looked like a thatched roof. My head was wrapped in a bandage, my right arm was in a sling, and everything hurt. There were two apparently indigenous Indian women standing at the foot of the bed, staring at me. Both were slim and slightly taller than the average South American natives you see in the movies, and both were...not unattractive. They had long, dark hair that fell almost to their waists, rich reddish skin, and wide black eyes, and they seemed...perceptive. That was, I hoped, the good news (it was a little early to tell).

I moaned and the women moved over quickly, with a handful of comforting words about being safe, and that it was best to relax for a while. One of them asked me how I was feeling. They were speaking Spanish, of sorts — it was a native dialect with several words I didn't get. But my Spanish was pretty good and I understood most of what was being said. (Maybe I was Spanish, or a native? I looked at my skin. Naahh, probably not...). Even more disconcerting was the fact that when I attempted a mumbling, almost unintelligible reply, I realized I still had no idea who I was. None whatsoever.

Later, when I regained consciousness once more, I was alone. I gradually, painfully, eased up to a sitting position and looked around. It was an odd room — the bed was small, the hand-woven sheets were clean, and there was a weathered bamboo bureau of sorts, over which my pants and shirt were draped. But the decorations on the walls were strange. They seemed to be an odd combination of Orthodox Catholicism — crosses with an unhappy Jesus on them. (Come to think of it, I didn't remember any "happy" Jesus pictures. Maybe that didn't matter. He was a busy fellow, with all that miracle-making stuff while constantly being chased by the Sheriff of Nottingham. No...wait...wrong story. Whew...I really wasn't doing well...)

It did seem to me that I had spoken with someone earlier — or *tried* to speak with someone...

I noticed there were paintings on the walls of conventional Christian sunrises, with a few angels here and there, along with oddly surrealistic depictions of what might be Hell. The hellish paintings had several devil-like fellows shown prominently — (short unobtrusive horns; wide, mostly smiling mouths; and transfixing eyes). It was very strange — an odd contradiction that left me feeling like somebody couldn't make up their mind.

I continued to rest. When I tried to move much, my body made it clear that was not high on the list yet. I was lying there, watching a lizard catch flies by the window, trying to remember... anything...when the two Indian women returned. They both knelt by the bed.

"How are you feeling, my husband?" said the slightly shorter one with the coal-colored, shorter hair and the full lips, as she leaned in and kissed me softly on my forehead, then found my lips briefly.

Now, that caught my attention because I knew I was certainly having some recall problems, but you'd think I might remember the "husband" thing. But she was quite nice...for a jungle maiden.

The other one (slightly taller; long, silky hair and pretty brown eyes) leaned in and kissed me on the cheek — her lips just sliding to the side of my mouth in the process, her hand running across my chest with just a touch of something that extended past sisterly concern. "We were so worried for you, lost in that terrible storm while hunting..." She eased out a sigh. "We found you in a deep gorge about an hour from the village. You must have fallen and banged your head..."

None of it sounded impossible, I supposed. But I couldn't remember a thing about anything. I felt like a clean slate... But I did notice that my skin was distinctly lighter than that of my ladies.

"I am Tosha," said the shorter of the two, stroking my face and diminishing my curiosity for the moment. "Do you not remember me, my husband?"

I drew a breath and looked at them, stared at them for a moment, trying desperately to get the gears of my brain to work. To remember. But everyone in my head was "out to lunch..." I tried...I really did. Tosha put her hand behind me and brought my head up while presenting me with a cup of tea-like liquid — nectarous and dark. "Drink and you will begin to feel better, I promise, my husband." She looked at me. "Do you remember your name?"

I shook my head slowly, trying to recall...*anything*... But there was still nothing but that blank wall.

"You are called Akawada a Dakak in our language," she replied. "But we call you Dakak to shorten..."

27

After a few swallows of the "tea," the other girl moved closer — sticky-sweet-smelling, silky hair falling on my chest as she leaned in. "How can you forget us, husband? How?" *Husband? Again? Phew... Two wives? Jesus!* It didn't seem like a bad thing, looking at them. But there was something about this whole thing that my head couldn't attach to.

The girl sighed as she laid her hand on my chest and moved in sensuously, her breath honeyed and warm. "I am Mika," she whispered with a vivacious light in her eyes. "I can't believe you could forget me. But not to worry, we will help you remember."

And for the next couple of days, I'll admit they did their best, and some of their methods were definitely entertaining. I was up and around a little now. They had quit feeding me like a baby chick, but I was still getting the magic potion to drink twice a day — to ease my pain and relieve my apprehension. But one of the big, obvious questions here still was...why did it appear I was the only white guy in the village? Even better, why was I the only guy? Or at least, that was the way it appeared.

When I asked about that, I was told there was "the old shaman of the village. But that is all the men," Mika answered with an indifferent shrug. "The gods get bored and do strange things," she added, sounding an awful lot like my old Rastaman friend, Rufus.

(Where did that come from? Who was Rufus?)

"The men..." She shrugged again. "They come and they go. We have found our need for them is not as great as some. We have found enjoyment in our independence and..." she smiled oddly, "our own company." Once again she dropped one of those smooth caramel shoulders. "Many moons ago we found you in the jungle and saved you from an ugly death. There was nothing with you that said who you were, or where you came from, so we took you home with us. Is that not good?" She grinned softly. "You seem to have a strange propensity for getting very lost. That is why you are called Akawada a Dakak."

I repeated the name. "It sounds almost regal. What does it mean?"

"Lost in jungle," she said with a smile. "Well, it actually means 'fool lost in jungle.'"

I drew back. "Really? Huh."

Mika shrugged. "It seemed appropriate at the time. But the gods must truly care about you because here you are again, safe…and mostly sound." She sighed gently and ran a soft hand across my brow. "Home again and safe. And that is good, no?"

When I got to feeling better, they did reintroduce me to their "friends" in the very small village — all women. Most of them had the soft, light-caramel color of my ladies, with long, dark hair that fell to their waists. Their wide eyes were a burnished ebony. *I still thought it was weird that in a tribe of over fifty people, there were no men, no boys…*

But given the fact that I still had no idea who I was, and I was operating on about fifty percent capacity, I let it pass. I was up and around now and feeling better. The strange brew they gave me morning and night seemed to help greatly. It took away all the sharp edges and left me damned near amused with life, but I still didn't know myself from squat. I mean, I was enjoying ant piles and sunsets a lot more than I could recall, when I could recall…and that juice definitely enhanced my ability to perform sexually with my two roomies. Man, sex, which they initiated almost immediately, was like Fourth of July stuff. But, through it all, there was still no one home at the inn. My memory just wasn't happening.

I noticed that the village sat below a large ridge/abutment that rose out between two hills above it. The earthen abutment seemed man-made, and I asked about it.

"It is what you call a *dam,"* said Mika. "Many years ago, when it rained hard for many days, the land-bowl above us would begin to fill with water, draining out at the point above the village. It was not disastrous but was…*inconvenient*, as you say. So we all worked one summer to build a dam to stop the process." She smiled proudly. "It was very difficult to build something so big but we did," she explained. "Much dirt it took — much dirt and rocks, and a whole summer. There is a small lake there now that we can fish, as well."

In the center of the village was what appeared to be a ceremonial circle, surrounded by a few interesting totems. There was a large, flat stone in the center. The stone seemed to be partially splashed with a dull, cherry-colored paint. It was odd, I had to admit. Another thing I did notice, in sort of an offhanded, indifferent fashion, was the mention of "a ceremony." It was spoken of in hushed tones with some anticipation. When I asked my "wives" about it, they exchanged a glance, then turned and grinned at me.

"Well, I guess there will be no surprising you," said Tosha. She smiled. "Yes, we will be having our annual village ceremony to appease our gods of Latima and Kata, for good fortune in the coming year. The gods have been kind to us this year. We must honor them." She paused. "We must give of ourselves with the same earnestness as the gods honor us." Sighing slightly, my new friend added, "It will be a wonderful honoring..." Tosha paused and her eyes became softly distant. She looked beautifully dedicated at that moment — like a priestess in the fading sunlight of an ancient temple. "There will be old breath for new breath, and old blood for new," she whispered. "It is the way..."

Mika smiled and kissed me passionately. "You will be such a blessing for this village." She paused and looked at me. "I suppose you should know that you will have the honor," she smiled lasciviously, "and the pleasure of playing an important role in the two-day ceremony. You see, it is primarily a fertility rite. The young women of the village gather together and 'open themselves' for the gift of life — you! We are your 'flowers.'" She smiled again. "And you will be 'the busy bee'..."

I took a step back and put up my hands. "Whoa...are you saying... You can't be saying..."

"Yes," said Tosha with a sensual grin. "You will pollinate our village so we will have new growth." She brought up a slender hand. "Actually, we are not the only village on this river of this 'ceremonial' persuasion. There is one other, to the north, that might also require your talents."

Well...you could have knocked me over with a condom...

I mean, on one hand, it was basically the dream of every guy from fourteen to...death. But man, there were at least thirty eligible females in that village.

I sighed, then brought my hands up again and smiled. "I mean, it sounds like a fun gig, and...I'd like to...help out... But it's just me, you know, and I'm likely to run out of..."

"Not to worry," said Mika. "You have been receiving a special potion in your daily drink that will enable a much-improved performance."

Ahhhh...yeah....

Damn, they'd thought of everything. Come to think of it, I had been feeling pretty...randy...lately. I paused for a moment and ran it by the ethics department one more time. (The truth was, drifting in the back of my mind somewhere was the knowledge of being "fixed." No kids for this old adventurer. Hmmm... Oh well, there would still be a good time had by all.)

I realized that this wasn't exactly ethical on my part. I mean, they weren't getting their money's worth. But the randy whore dog in me just couldn't resist. What a barroom story! Besides, there was a part of me that said if I told them the truth, I might find myself cast out of the village like a rug-peeing dog. Just me and the jungle... I shrugged and smiled. "I guess a man's gotta do what a man's gotta do, huh?"

I didn't sleep well that night, even with the ministrations of the girls. I couldn't help thinking about the ceremony coming up. Nope — I wasn't telling these folks shit about my amorous limitations. I'd have a good time, then rent a canoe and a guide, and paddle downriver until I saw a Coca-Cola sign.

There was one other thing that set me back slightly. I had a dream that night. At least, it seemed like a dream. I saw an older man — suntanned, a patch over one eye, long blond hair sticking out from the famous ball cap he claimed Jimmy Buffett had given him. *(How did I know that?)* He was standing in the doorway of my room, dressed in what seemed to be his usual tropical shirt and blue jeans. He stood there for a moment, staring at me. Then he offered a distant smile and touched two fingers to his cap sadly, and the next moment, he was gone. I wanted to say...Ed. It was a bit unnerving. No, it was *a lot* unnerving.

But about that time, life took another of those quantum leaps it so often seemed to do for me, and I was forced to pay attention to the present. I remembered a saying from someone...probably Rufus? *"Dere be nothin' dat de gods can't do, and if you bore dem enough, dey will."*

The following day, I was sitting on the small porch of the hut when two of the tribe's "hunters" returned from an early morning foray. But behind them, they dragged in a guest. He was battered,

31

bruised, and dirty, his clothes were ripped to shreds, but strangely enough, it appeared he was a white guy like myself.

As they brought him in, I was some distance away, but I stared at the bedraggled, muddy figure. About then he stopped and wavered, exhausted, in the center of the village — tall and skinny, with blue eyes and a wide mouth, his longish blond hair a bird's nest. And all of a sudden, my jaw dropped. The specter gradually surveyed the area and came to a stop when he saw me. Suddenly, his eyes went wide and he slowly straightened up. He pointed a wavering finger at me. "Kansas!" he croaked. "Holy shit! Kansas!"

Our mouths fell open and as the veils of time and circumstance dropped away, we both broke into astonished grins. *I couldn't believe my eyes!* At that moment, there was a sudden avalanche in my head. A million thoughts came pouring in. A thousand memories surfaced all at one time.

I remembered! Good God! I remembered!

I recalled everything in a psychedelic rush. The plane going down. My friends. Eddie. The kids. Parachuting out into the night... My son, Tax! And my dog, Shadow! Where in heaven's name were they? Where were my boys?

In the next instant, my friend and I were stumbling at each other, grappling with disbelief and gratitude as my mind exploded with memories. "Son of a bitch," I whispered. "Will! Will! Damn. There is a God. There sure as hell is a God!"

Our feminine villagers thought we were both mad. But they didn't really care. It didn't change their plans. In fact, it enhanced them.

Now, I know you're shaking your head and saying that this kind of coincidence is just a little over the top. And I know some of the things that have happened to me seem like barroom bullshit, but I am damned sure that my old Jamaican friend, Rufus, is right. I remember him saying, *"Most people, dey jus' bore de gods shitless. Dere be way too many lifeless, useless people on dis spinning ball of dirt and water dat have never 'thrown da dice' in dere entire lives. But every once in a while, mon, de gods find a soul or two who make life interesting, and de damned truth is, I tink dey go out of dere way to preserve dese folks as best dey can. Because everybody need some entertainment, even da gods…"*

Besides, the truth was, I now remembered watching Will's chute as we fell out of the stormy sky, and how I tried to stay with him then, as much as possible, given the circumstances. I saw him go into the jungle about a half mile from where I had touched down and slammed into the tree. The women hunters in the tribe said they had trails that ran for miles around the village. It wasn't that much of a stretch of the imagination that they had found Will. It was lucky, for sure, but then luck was an old acquaintance of ours.

Will was seriously roughed up and had missed a few meals, and he smelled like the south end of a northbound baboon, but by all accounts, nothing was permanently bunged up. I hugged him again, then pushed him back. "Damn, buddy, you stink! But damn! I'm so glad to see you! There isn't any chance you've seen anything of Tax or Jing, huh? Or Shadow? Or Eddie?"

Will shook his head sadly. "No…nothing. But if we survived, there's a chance they did too. That's what we've gotta hold on to."

"Ya, mon," I whispered. "Where there's breath, there's hope." I smiled mischievously. "The good news is, your timing is great. You need a shave and a bath for sure, but we're about to have a special ceremony in this village tomorrow, and I'm thinking you're going to be included as a guest of honor."

My buddy smiled. "Guest of honor, huh?"

I held up my hands and smiled. "You got no idea…"

"Yeah, yeah, that sounds great," muttered Will, pushing me back. "Now, you guys got anything to eat here?"

I grinned. "Sure, sure. But let's get you cleaned up a bit before the girls get back."

My filthy friend perked up. "Girls? *Girls?"*

I couldn't help but smile. "Oohh, ya mon… Ya mon!" I held up a hand. "But don't get too relaxed. This is just a train stop. We need to be on our way, soon…" And again I thought of my son, Tax, and Shadow. Could they still be alive? Lord, we needed to be on our way. But in all truth, Will needed a day or two to recuperate, and leaving now would just be bad manners.

Later that afternoon — after Will received the attention of a couple of village girls down at the river and got "seriously clean" — my buddy and I decided to try for a little insight from the only other male in the village — the old shaman. He had, throughout my visit, distinctly avoided me. My girls were still gone for the afternoon, visiting a nearby village, so I decided to take a chance because we needed some information. A recon, you might say. It was an interesting meeting.

The shaman — long gray hair; a grizzled beard; reddish, withered skin; large, dark eyes that indeed looked like they held a secret or two — confirmed in broken Spanish the "pollination party" we were going to have. Sure enough, it was a "screw until you drop" kind of thing — a lot like a college weekend.

It was certainly intriguing on one hand, for a couple of old whore-dogs like Will and me, but even through the excitement we felt, there was something just slightly out of place in the old man's eyes. I couldn't quite touch it. Yeah…through it all there was a certain melancholy that draped him.

"You have lived a good life, a full life, yes?" he asked.

He sounded like he was preparing a eulogy.

We glanced at each other and shrugged.

"Yeah," I said. "Damned good, actually."

Will offered an affirmative. "Ya mon…too true."

The shaman nodded again. "That is wonderful. It is well that you come to us." The elderly man paused and sighed. "Old breath for new breath, and old blood for new," he whispered. "It is the way…"

Hmmm… I remembered hearing Mika and Tosha (my wives who weren't really my wives, I now knew) using that same expression in a somewhat reverent fashion.

Then the guy seemed to pull out of the melancholy dive. He stared at us for a moment and offered a weary smile again. "Live for the moment," he whispered, bringing up his hands. "Live every minute of the next two days of ceremony, for they will be remarkable, even for men like you. You will bring life to us, and the village will be…beholden."

So, that was exactly what my partner and I decided to do. And it was, even for adventurers and tail-chasers like us, extraordinary.

I did, however, confront my "wives" about them not being my wives, and they apologized profusely, explaining that their deception was only used because their village was desperate for a quality infusion of "maleness." And being as handsome and healthy as I was... So, naturally, I could see where they might be tempted...with a guy like me... So I let it all slide.

The first day of the ceremony began innocuously, with a parade of the village's eligible females moving down to the river to bathe...to get plenty clean and shiny for "the festivities."

Will and I sat on the sandy bluff just above them and watched — velvet-skinned, reddish-tanned goddesses of all sizes, laughing and splashing in the sunlit water. I tell you what, after that show, I would have done just fine without the "special juice." But it was sort of a preamble to the night's activities.

Will and I drank the rum punches we'd been given in coconuts (spiked with more of the "wanger medicine," I was sure). It was a nice start to what would be an impossibly memorable experience for us.

But by the end of the first night, I didn't know how another day would be possible. I felt like the only whore on a ship of randy sailors.

The only out-of-the-ordinary development at that point was, apparently, a small earth tremor. When Will and I were sitting, watching the parading, frolicking girls with unabashed drooling, the ground began to tremble slightly. It wasn't exactly shaking, just vibrating some, but it was still enough to make things move a bit, and it was certainly enough to create a little concern on our part. The girls quickly explained that it was just Tongo, their main god, sneezing, and it would pass without issue. They were right. It did. But I had watched the huts and the hills around the village tremble slightly.

Will, ever the official "explainer of things," defined it as a minor earthquake. He added that this area (the tip of South America) was geologically prone to earth movements, but anything serious was probably fifty or a hundred years out yet.

I eased out a breath of relief. It didn't matter to us, we weren't staying. After one more day of "community service," we were booking a canoe downriver and getting out of town.

But by morning, and another coconut or two of the wanger go-go juice (which made Viagra look like rabbit food), Will and I were once again the most popular people in the village. It was truly incredible but by afternoon, our hosts realized that even with the special tonic, the two white boys might need a little break. So, it was jointly decided that we could sleep for a few hours in the afternoon, and eat something to keep our energy up. Then we'd start the party again, in the evening.

We might have continued blindly along on this voyage of extraordinary sexual madness if it hadn't been for a visit from the old shaman.

There was a knock at the bamboo door. Will and I were alone. Tosha and Mika had gone down to the river to bathe. Still blurry-eyed and dizzy from practically mainlining sex, booze, and wanger juice, I staggered to the door, and there was the local witch doctor, no shirt, a worn leather jerkin, and a ragged pair of Hang Ten shorts. *(I had to wonder who those belonged to originally...)* I let him in and he stared at us for a moment, then sighed heavily and brought up his wrinkled hands. "I cannot let this happen again..." he said in his broken Spanish.

Happen again? That didn't make me happy, exactly.

"I am shamed that I must break my vows with my village," he croaked passionately. "I am an old man," he muttered, as if talking to himself, "and I am not fond of the idea of finding death before it is supposed to find me. But my conscience burns holes in my head." He stared at us. "You must leave this evening, before the final 'midnight ceremony'. You must flee...slip away, take one of the canoes by the river and head toward the sea. But tell no one of this conversation."

Will, ever the horn-dog, held out his hands. "Why? Why should we leave? Our people love us!" he said with a smile. "I mean, *really* love us. This is like a story out of *Playboy Magazine*. I'll be telling this tale in bars twenty years from now."

"He's right, why should we leave early?" I added.

The shaman sighed. "All right, I will tell you because you are blind pigs who will never find the acorn by yourselves." Again, he eased out a breath. "I risk my life talking to you," he growled. "But I am old...and bored... I will tell you a story but it does not have a happy ending." He paused and held up a grizzly, bent forefinger. "A man forewarned..." With another heavy exhale he began to talk about spiders. "The Brazilian black widow fornicates many times

36

with its mate," he explained, staring at us as he spoke. "She is extremely passionate, and the pleasure is greatly shared with the male."

"Seems like fun," I said.

The old man fixed me with a stare, then continued. "But when they are finished and the male is resting, exhausted, she pounces on him and kills him. Some say so he can't tell anyone of her new offspring. Some say because she has what she wants now, and he no longer matters…" He stared at us for a moment longer, making sure we understood, and the room got quiet. "This is the fifth 'New Blood Ceremony' I have witnessed since I came to this village many, many moons ago. I have seen much sacrifice and much birth in that time, and the village has survived, but the males have not."

I blanched. "Are you saying…" I looked out at the central square and the women occupied with their chores, many of them watching our hut, waiting. "You don't mean…that these girls would screw us, then…" I shrugged. "C'mon, they wouldn't hurt us… really… Hell, if you're telling the truth, why are *you* still here?"

"I am the shaman," he growled with a wave of his hand. "I am older than dirt and am no threat…or use…to anyone, and I satisfy their needs as a conduit to the gods. But mostly now, I am just an old man who sits in the sun." He threw another harsh glance at us. "Have you not heard them whisper of…" He held out his hands. "…the fertility rite?' Surely you have."

Well, not exactly…not in so many words. But the big, mostly ignored question had been, where were the men or the boys in this village? A question that was always shuffled off with a shrug or an empty explanation. This whole thing was a little like a Rod Serling movie.

The old guy looked at me as if reading my mind. "Yes…where are the males? Huh?" He shook his head. "Every place of refuge has its price."

"An Eagles fan," mumbled Will. "He can't be all bad." My friend cleared his throat. "So, you're actually telling us that after they/we get screwed to our hearts' content…" He paused.

The old man nodded solemnly, eyes hard with ugly knowledge. "As sure as the ripe mango drops. How else would a village of all girls and women exist? I ask you, how would it be possible?" He paused and stared at us darkly. "They do not keep the male babies. They have not for over fifty years."

Will huffed out a gasp. "Sounds like the *Twilight Zone*, dude! We need to pack a bag, man, and book a jungle taxi."

"Yes, you do. *Now*," said the shaman. "I have risked myself enough." He sighed. "For what, I do not know — idiots, I think."

"You're on my Christmas card list, dude," said Will. "If nothing else."

In the next minute, the old man was gone, slipping away like smoke...

My buddy looked at me. "Well, this is a fine mess you've gotten us into, Ollie!"

In the distance, through the window, I could see the sun easing into the hills of the jungle, and the shadows had begun to creep across the village. Somewhere in the back of my head, I could hear the lyrics of an old Three Dog Night hit.

This is the craziest party that could ever be.
Don't turn on the lights 'cause I don't wanna see...
Mama told me not to come. Mama told me not to come.

"Okay, this is how I see it," I said nervously. "We go ahead and start the party, but well before midnight, while everyone is loose and close to stupid drunk, we make a run for the beach."

Neither of us actually thought the old village shaman was exactly right in his assumptions, but we couldn't afford to be wrong, so we were booking a midnight canoe.

"Get your gear together," said Will. "I'll pack a lunch."

I shook my head. "Nobody's ever gonna believe this."

"Shit," muttered Will. "Hardly matters. They haven't believed half of what we've told them already."

We packed a gunny sack of food — bread, fruit, and some unidentifiable smoked meat from the girls' wooden pantry, and hid it under the back porch of the little shack. Then we both took a breath and knocked down another cup of wanger juice each.

"Time to get back to the party — before they come looking for us," I said.

Will exhaled, got that goofy half-grin of his, and said, "A man's gotta do what a man's gotta do…"

As concerned and intrigued as I was with this situation, I couldn't help being drawn back to the kids…and Eddie — old Crazy Eddie. We had to get out of there — we had to find our family and our friend and my dog,

The sun had barely set and the moon was rising, and we were back in full swing. I mean, it was something that the average teenager would leverage up in wet dreams. Many of these women were really quite attractive, and very anxious to please. But the truth was, we were winding way down, even with all erotica and the wanger juice, and most of the village was too drunk to care. Will and I had just said good night to two quite attractive ladies in one of the huts. They were leaving when my friend turned to me and whispered, "I think it's time to boogie, dude. Slip out the back, Jack. Make a new plan, Stan…"

"Yeah, yeah," I hissed. "I get it. I get it."

I looked around. It was just the two of us and an empty hut — sleeping mats, food bowls, daily equipment, and utensils.

"We need a distraction," I muttered.

Will thought about it for a moment, then pulled out a Bic lighter. "Nothing like some smoke and fire to get people's attention." He moved over, bent down, and lit the back corners of the hut. The dry bamboo and sawgrass sucked at the flames like greedy lovers. In just a few moments, we had a situation. As the flames licked up the interior sides, Will and I stumbled out, yelling "Fire! Fire!"

"Fire" is one of the words, in any language, that absolutely catches the attention of people who live in grass huts. In just moments, the women were dragging over strategically placed containers of water and throwing the contents on the smoking hut. But the ravenous orange flames were already reaching out toward another of the adjacent accommodations. The women were very efficient, and it looked like they would control the fire, but it did have the village occupied for the moment.

Will and I casually eased ourselves back into the shadows, then quickly headed for the girls' residence and our supplies. From there it would be just a dash to the beach and a canoe.

I don't necessarily like coincidence but I believe in it — both good and bad — depending entirely on the mood of the gods, as Rufus would say.

Suddenly, out from the shadows stepped our two ladies and a couple of their friends. All of them carried large knives.

"I wish you would have been a little more cooperative," said Mika. "Your 'passing' could have been so easy for you." She sighed and brought up her knife. "Not so messy…"

"Nothing has to be messy," said Will, holding up his hands, palms out. "We've already given you what you want, pretty much. We'll just be on our way. Everybody wins…"

Mika shook her head sadly. "No, the gods must win." She held her knife almost sadly, but determined. "They must have the blood that they are due."

"Maybe we could flip a coin — you just take one of us and let the other go…" pleaded Will.

"Hell no!" I cried. "He's got a trick coin and I get screwed, more…again!"

My partner was about to try another tack, but at that moment, the ground began to tremble again. This time, it was more than just a little tremor. This time, it hammered the surrounding earth hard enough to cost everyone their balance.

"Not good," muttered Will, rising to his feet and glancing around nervously.

The women's eyes went hard as they pulled themselves up and began to gather around us. They chanted harshly in unison — very spooky. But the gods weren't done. At that moment, there was a ripping, thunderous bellow from inside the earth and we were all shaken completely off our feet again. The ground around us began to roll and tremble, and the bamboo floor of the hut popped and cracked. The rafters and the short stilts of the flimsy house gave and it began to collapse in on itself. Will and I were close to the kitchen doorway that led to the back. In a blink, we were on our way out, stumbling down the short stairs and grabbing our gear. The women were following when the earth did another rolling explosion and the hut collapsed.

But that wasn't the worst of it. I looked up and realized that the old earthen dam that held back the lake above the village was breaching — splitting and crumbling — and the several tons of water it contained were starting to surge out and down the slope, right at the encampment.

"A canoe!" I screamed, grabbing my friend. "A canoe!"

And in the next moment, we were racing down the slight slope from the village to the river. I could hear the cries and screams succumbing to the roar of the waters, and bouncing around in my head I could hear the quote of an old bandit we'd once met on a gig in Mexico... *"Pandemonium is the devil's favorite tune..."*

There was no question. The dam above the village from heaven and hell was giving way, crumbling at the center. As the earth shook beneath our feet again, water was spilling over the top and pulling away the dirt and stones that had held it together for over thirty years. People were screaming and running in all directions, but I was beginning to realize that one of the most popular directions was the river and the canoes.

"C'mon, man!" I yelled, grabbing my partner by his shirt and pulling him toward the river.

Glancing around, I couldn't see any of "our women" and their friends, and that was just fine with me. We were running out of time. The center of the dam was going, and the river was still fifty yards away. For some reason, in the back of my head, all I could hear were the lyrics of Paul Simon:

> *Slip out the back, Jack.*
> *Make a new plan, Stan.*
> *You don't need to be coy Roy, just get yourself free.*

And indeed that was the plan but there were a couple of problems for Jack and Stan...and us. While we were a little ahead of a lot of the village, those damned women were some fast runners. My buddy and I got to the shore and the canoes about thirty seconds ahead of the horde of whores, and many of them were carrying knives and screaming. I didn't know if they were just pissed that we had beaten them to the river, or if they just wanted to make sure "the ceremony" was completed. I didn't care. We were snatching a canoe and getting out of town.

The good news was, we grabbed a canoe with two paddles, jumped in, and started rowing like gerbils on cocaine. The bad news was the dam. It suddenly gave way with a rumbling groan, and while the surge of water tumbling out wasn't Biblical (it was only about three or four feet high), it still rolled across the village, taking out huts and cooking fires and drying racks like the wave of a giant's hand. Fortunately, most of the women had made it to the river, and by the time the wave reached the water, it had diminished some. But it still threw people out into the water, overturning canoes and casting flotsam and jetsam across the surface of the muddy green flow.

Fortunately for Will and me, this wasn't our first canoe ride and we weathered things pretty well. By the time we had some degree of control, we were headed well downriver toward the coast and away from the Venezuelan Sodom and Gomorrah.

Looking back at the slightly scorched, water-inundated village, I felt a degree of empathy for the occupants. I looked over at Will, who was gazing back at the ravaged village as well. I sighed. "I feel kind of sorry for them...I mean, they've lost a lot..."

My partner shook his head. "Yeah, it'll take a little while before they get everything back in order...and can coax in another couple of suckers, yank 'em until they're raw, then kill them unmercifully."

"Hmm. Yeah, point taken." I smiled. "Slip out the back, Jack..."

Will grinned. "Make a new plan, Stan..."

For the next few hours, we paddled along leisurely with the current toward the coast and civilization, I hoped. As we drifted in an almost peaceful fashion, watching the incredibly colorful birds scatter through the trees like bright confetti, the monkeys effortlessly soaring from branch to branch, and the crocodiles sunbathing on logs and riverbanks, I had a few minutes to take in all that had happened to us in the last few days. It was all simply incredible. Another one of those bar stories that no one was going to believe. But beyond our situation, I couldn't help but wonder and agonize over what had happened to the rest of our people — Tax and Jing especially, and Shadow and Eddie...

As he did so often, Will read my mind. "The kids..." he whispered. "I wonder where they are..." He just looked at me. Then his eyes fell away toward the muddy water.

"And Eddie," I said. I couldn't bring myself to speculate on our

42

old friend. I had a terrible feeling in my chest when I thought about him.

CHAPTER FIVE

In one of the many small miracles that had occurred during the night of the storm, Shadow managed to reach the trunk of a fallen banyan tree near the shore. Its roots had been undermined by the current, and the main trunk of the tree had cascaded into the river. He clawed his way up through the branches to the trunk and lay across it, panting, gasping, just inches above the water. After about ten minutes, the dog began to claw his way along the battered torso of the tree to the shore. Shadow crawled into the thick jungle at the edge of the river and it offered a little protection from the storm. He lay there, shivering from exhaustion, terrified at the brutal separation from his lifelong friend, and frightened by the uncertainty that faced him, until daylight, when a wan sun broke through the foliage. That was the good news.

Then there was the bad...

Two hundred yards away, a big male jaguar lifted itself from the heavy branch of a giant rubber tree. The cat's head rose slowly and its nostrils flared. There was a new smell in the air, not far away. The jaguar's stomach growled as he balanced on the single limb with practiced ease, head up. *Yes, there was something different in the air — and it smelled...intriguing...*

The dog gave himself a half hour to recover. During that time, the simple, basic process of survival began to kick in. And indeed, Shadow was a survivor. He was a tough customer in a fight. The dog was in his prime now, a shepherd/Rottweiler mix, heavy and muscled, and his powerful jaws could snap a two-by-two without effort. And he had killed before, to save his master's life. Moreover, he was raised with the latitude to be as much as he could be. He was not just *a dawg* that lay in the dirt outside a trailer. He had been brought up as a companion. He had been taught to use his mind to survive, as well as his jaws.

Nonetheless, he was at a disadvantage here — lost, hungry, and disoriented. In the back of his mind, there was a simple effort of concern. *Where was his friend...Kansas? And where was the winged creature with which he shared a strange bond?*

The jaguar balanced on the heavy limb and surveyed everything around him. The sun was just working its way through the motley gray sheets of clouds above the horizon. The cat sniffed again. *It was still there. That smell…* He coughed angrily. *Nothing entered his domain without his permission. Besides, he was hungry…* He crouched on the branch, then casually, effortlessly fluid, leapt to the jungle floor. His head rose as he took in the scent one more time, then he set off after it.

Shadow pulled himself to his feet and shook hard, throwing off the water that weighted down his coat. He raised his head and studied his surroundings. Nothing was familiar but the area was rich with sounds and scents — the chatter and caws of birds, the distant screeching of monkeys, the odor of scat from small and large animals, and the occasional grunt or cough of bigger competition. He glanced around once more, looking upstream, then downstream. His muzzle came up and he sniffed the air again. There was a slight notion of salt air to the north, and to the south was a rise of mountains. He chose the easy path, the one that took him toward the sea. With caution, he moved out along the edge of the angry river.

Unfortunately, his actions didn't go unobserved. Just inside the jungle, the jaguar watched him, focused on one of those "creatures" he often found in the villages. But the cat wasn't concerned. He had nearly a hundred pounds on the animal, and twice the armament. It would make a good meal that could carry him for days.

Slowly, as the sun broke over the distant mountains to his back, Shadow began easing himself along the river. He carried more savvy and insight than most animals. He was intellectually capable to the very cusp of his species. He moved out with growing confidence.

But the creature that was now tracking him was a killing machine. The big male was nearly two hundred fifty pounds, with four and five-inch talons on its calloused feet. It possessed blinding speed, and heavy, powerful jaws fitted with razor-sharp, dagger-like incisors. It lived to kill, and it was very good at it.

Shadow cautiously followed the twisting river, allowing himself a drink on occasion, constantly paying attention to his periphery. He had no idea how far he had to go. He wasn't hungry yet. Too much had happened and his adrenaline was still high. As he moved along, he was entertained by a collage of jungle animals, from howler monkeys, who chattered angrily at him from the treetops, to large sloths, and huge river otters that splashed like playful puppies along the riverbank. Then there were the snakes and colorful lizards, which by instinct and some history, he avoided. If he wasn't so concerned about his human friend, it would have been...enjoyable. Oddly enough, his thoughts also drifted to the bird creature...*hawk?* Which, in some strange fashion that even he didn't understand, had become his companion. In the Keys, when his master, Kansas, visited the female called Jing, Shadow and her incredible winged creature would often disappear for hours along the mangrove shorelines. They possessed a bond that most humans would have said was almost impossible, or at the very least, uncanny.

The truth is, most people have little or no real understanding of animals. I'm reminded of the quote by naturalist Henry Beston: *"In a world older and more consummate than ours, they moved finished and complete, gifted with the extension of the senses we have lost or never attained, living by voices we shall never hear. They are not brethren, they are not underlings: they are other nations, caught with ourselves in the net of life and time, fellow prisoners through the splendour and travail of the earth."*

While Shadow moved at a steady but somewhat leisurely pace along the river, the big cat followed, gradually moving in. But during that same time, there was another scenario taking place about a half mile upriver.

Silvano Petros — boatsman, pirate, smuggler, and sometimes, when absolutely necessary, trader of things he had "acquired" here and there — sat at the helm of a somewhat battered, converted trawler that he called home. The truth was, he was an entertaining fellow, and the gold and diamond miners and some of the villages along the Tuy River and its tributaries did look forward to his occasional visits. The original outriggers were gone, and aside from often carrying oddities that made life better (good knives, coffee, sugar, flour, some ammunition, *Playboy* magazines, and most importantly, news from along the river), Silvano had stories that could raise your hair or burst your belly with laughter.

No one could ever tell where the truth ended and imagination took over, but it hardly mattered, and the pirate played the mandolin with a deftness that could make the old miners cry. But like everyone said, it was great to have him as a visitor but you wouldn't want him as a neighbor, and you needed to count your fingers and check your women when he left.

Actually, Silvano was a displaced, possibly disowned Italian, whose parents had come to South America to work for the burgeoning railroad system. He was only three years old when they arrived. He was five when his father was killed in a railroad accident. In less than a year, his mother died of helplessness, raw poverty, and a broken heart. Silvano would have most likely died along with her (which was common for abandoned children in those days), but a nun from a local mission (the Mother of Hope Mission in the town of Maiquetia on the coast), found him in an alley, starving and neglected, and too weak physically and spiritually to care.

"An act of God," he called it later, and it probably was.

There was no question that they saved him. There also was no question that he wasn't particularly fond of his salvation — too much regimentation, too little food, too much God. Every day, pray, pray, pray… Some people are just destined to be who they are, no matter how much people try to fix that. There was no question that Silvano Petros was a hooligan from the onset and that he lacked any serious conscience. But he had a penchant for animals. He had been allowed to keep a small cat he found in the street. It became his friend and his confidant. The rebellious boy and the abandoned gray feline became inseparable friends. The only time he ever cried in his life was when the cat died, just before he left the mission.

Silvano, ragtag rascal and part villain that he was, never forgot that he was saved by the nuns of the Mother of Hope Mission. He always said when he became rich, he would repay them, but he never quite got around to being rich.

The old Italian kept a big old tomcat on board — to help keep the varmint population down, he said. But those who knew him said he could often be heard in earnest conversation with that furry companion, and when no one was watching, on those long days and nights along the river, you might well find that cat in his lap.

As the Italian boatsman/bandit worked his way down the Guaire River, one of Venezuela's fairly significant waterways, Shadow continued his course toward the coast, along the shore, but the big cat was still closing in behind him. As the dog came to a small circular clearing by the river, he moved to the water for a drink. The jaguar was now circling in the darkness of the jungle, getting as close as possible before he struck. There was simply no question to this outcome. The dog had struggled through much — he had been a survivor, but there is no justice in the jungle. Almost every creature sees the same fate. Eventually, you die ugly.

Shadow was at the water's edge and was drinking thirstily just as Silvano Petros rounded the bend in the river, studying the foliage on both sides — always a good practice in a place of bandits and predators of all sorts. Suddenly, his eyes went wide. There in front of him was a large dog, drinking at the shore, and for just a few seconds the animal had let his guard down. At that moment, out from the foliage to his left sprang a spotted tan thunderbolt — death on claws. The Italian sucked in a breath. The dog turned, suddenly aware of his plight, but didn't flee. It swung to face its assailant, instantly bristled, hackles up, teeth bared.

Silvano stood there. His jaw dropped and his eyes widened in disbelief. The dog had no chance, not a chance in hell, and every other animal he had ever seen or known would have instantly turned and run, but not this one. It braced itself, facing death with an angry pride like nothing the little Italian had ever seen.

"*Oddio! Mannaggia!*" he hissed in Italian. "Such pride and courage..." he whispered as he watched death come to the dog. He couldn't pull his eyes away.

But at that moment, the most amazing thing Petros had ever seen took place. He would tell the story for years to come. No one ever believed it. It was almost too much for the old pirate — and he lied for pleasure.

The jaguar was out of the jungle in a tan blur. The dog still stood its ground, teeth bared, a roar coming up from his big chest. But he had no chance in this contest. In the last dozen feet, the cat sprang into the air, literally flying at the dog, front legs extended, those deadly claws out and exposed.

Still, the dog refused to run. It stood there, the image of gallantry and fearlessness, exemplifying the very meaning of courage and epitomizing the pride that is found in every great story in history — from the Greeks who perished at the pass of Thermopylae against the Persian Army to the two hundred incredible men who died hard at the Alamo so Texas could exist. For just a moment, that damned dog stood for the hero in all of us, and Silvano Petros just couldn't believe his eyes.

Just when the older man thought he was watching the impossible, the whole thing got more outrageous. Even as the cat was in the air, there was a shadow above him, and as the sun lit the scene it defined the impossible. It was a hawk, a huge osprey, falling from the sky like a clawed meteor and hammering the cat, which was in midair as well. The jaguar screamed with surprise and pain as the hawk's talons found his head and his right eye, and the two of them tumbled completely out of control in midair, then crashed to the ground. Now, as if things couldn't get any more outrageous (and in the back of Petros's head, he was already thinking what a tale this was going to make around the campfire), the dog, rather than running, charged in and tore at the cat, giving the hawk a chance to free itself and become airborne again, but paying a price for his bravery as the jaguar pinned him for a moment and its claws found his side.

Silvano couldn't believe his eyes. The dog harried the cat long enough for the osprey to break free, then both of them retreated in tandem — the dog backing up to the trunk of a big rubber tree and the bird landing on a branch above him.

"*Madre de Dios,*" whispered the old pirate, switching to Spanish as the big cat, who had probably lost an eye, shuffled backward, hissing in painful anger. The dog growled and moved forward slightly, bristled and angry — no surrender in him whatsoever, and the hawk above him screamed in defiance, bringing those huge wings up and out, preparing to swoop down in attack again.

"*Madre de Dios! No es posible...*" whispered the Italian, as the cat hissed again in pain and frustration, then suddenly turned and disappeared into the jungle in a blur.

"*Magnifica,*" the old riverman muttered as he shook his head in amazement. *"Simplemente magnifica!"*

It was an absolutely remarkable happening, which looked like it had ended fairly well, but it was then that he saw the blood draining along the dog's ribcage. The animal had been running on adrenaline, but with the cat gone, he had slowed. He was hurt badly.

It was then that the whole affair took one more step into the impossible. Silvano watched as the big osprey lifted its wings and sailed off the branch and down to the ground, next to the dog, almost touching it. It chirped softly and moved a little closer, and the huge dog lifted its muzzle and ran a long pink tongue across the back of the bird. Then it eased back down with a sigh.

"Ooohhh, *mi Dios,*" Silvano whispered incredulously again. "Nobody ever gonna believe me when I tell this. Nobody... They jus' think I be a stinkin' drunk liar...and I am. But..."

And yet there was more to come.

Silvano realized that the dog was seriously wounded. He could see the stain of blood growing on the animal's side. When the creature moved, a flap of skin lay open and he could see the paleness of exposed ribs and the pulsing of blood.

"Ooohh, *Dios...*" he whispered, knowing that at the very least, the wound needed to be closed and bandaged or the dog could bleed to death. And also knowing that the chances of getting away with that and not ending up looking like hamburger from the ministrations of the hawk or the dog, were slim.

Silvano exhaled heavily, making a decision. He quickly pulled his dinghy into the stern and climbed aboard, then headed for shore. In moments, he was pulling his little boat up on the bank and moving cautiously to the dog.

The man crouched and studied the dog for a moment. He exhaled again, then rose and moved a little closer. The wolf-dog studied him as he approached and the hawk took to the air again, circling tightly above him and calling angrily. The old Italian slowly knelt by the wounded animal and gently whispered to him, promising to help. The hawk landed a few feet away, chirping angrily, its eyes glaring, promising bad things.

The Italian took another breath and gambled his fingers, reaching out tentatively and stroking the canine for a few moments, talking quietly and studying the wound. The dog's skin had been torn loose in a spot about six inches wide. There were claw marks in the flesh and the scarred whiteness of the ribs showed slightly. Given the pain the dog appeared to be in, there could be internal damage as well. The animal had bled quite a bit, his fur was soaked red on his side and stomach, but the bleeding seemed to have slowed. The old man would have to treat and close the wound, and bandage it to keep away infection.

Silvano spoke quietly to the canine, explaining that he would have to go back to the boat for his medical kit. He knew the uselessness of that effort, but he didn't know what else to do. As he got into his dinghy and headed back to his boat, he realized there was a good chance the dog (and the bird) would be gone when he returned, the dog doing what creatures tended to do when wounded badly — slip away to a hole somewhere and lick their wounds clean…or die.

Nonetheless, when the Italian returned, the dog and the bird were still there. For the next half hour, he carefully cleaned and treated the animal as best he could — checking the ribs, pinching off a severed vein with some thread, and closing the wound — basically, putting the flap of fur back in place with a couple of simple stitches and hoping it would catch. He then wrapped the dog's abdomen with strips of a sheet. The dog had lost a lot of blood and was in "wound shock" to some degree, which probably explained its docile cooperation. It would need time to recover.

To Silvano's amazement, the sea hawk never left the dog. It stood silently off to the side at first, those hard, dark eyes following the Italian's every move. Then it opted for a branch in the tree above them, where it could watch and protect more efficiently. The man, sitting by the dog, looked up at the hawk and shook his head in amazement. He turned to his patient. "You got an amazing *amigo*, *perro. Incredibile…*"

If you asked him why, Silvano probably couldn't have given you an acceptable answer because it wasn't his nature to go out of his way for others, but Señor Petros stayed with the dog (and the hawk) throughout the morning and part of the afternoon, watching for big cats. Although he hadn't voiced it in particular, it could have been he stayed because he had witnessed something that struck a place deep in his core — courage and integrity, and friendship so profound that it trumped life itself. He had just watched two creatures offer their very lives to protect each other. They weren't of the same family, or even the same species, yet they willingly offered themselves up to fate to safeguard one another. It was like something in the books that his mother used to read to him, and it struck a place in the man that he thought had died. *If you spend your entire life worrying about nothing but yourself, in the end all you have is yourself.*

Silvano Petros always said that it was gods, guns, and money that motivated this spinning ball of dirt and water, and he probably wasn't far from wrong. But no amount of cleverness or illusion or deft maneuvering could buy what Silvano had seen today — friendship, and yes, even love, that trumped death itself. *"Sonabitche,"* he whispered incredulously. *"Sonabitche..."*

As Señor Petros stared out at the afternoon sun, he was struck by a small epiphany. He had nothing but a piece-of-shit boat, the contents of which he had wrangled by guile or had stolen. He had nothing like what he had just witnessed — no one who cared about him enough to offer peace of mind in times of need, or healing in times of pain, or refuge in the last moments of life. Yes, he had hoarded away a few gems recently, and he had a few coins that had been wrangled or stolen and hidden on a battered craft that could sink at any time, and he had thought of himself as clever...

It was a weird damned thing, to be given an epiphany in such a fashion, and it wasn't like he was ready to commit himself to a monastery and become a priest. But something in his psyche had been heated and reshaped, and now it would have to cool to see if the new form held. Petros shrugged, staring out at the river. "Who knows?" he whispered to the breeze as he turned and studied the falling sun. He took another draw from his *cigarillo* and let it out slowly, thoughtfully. Somewhere in the back of his head, he remembered a quote from his mother... *Until one has loved an animal, a part of one's soul remains unawakened...*

He looked at the two creatures, then he slowly moved over and eased himself down next to the dog. He paused for a second, then whispered, "Come, my friend, do not fear me. It is my turn to give a little..."

The dog looked up at him with pain-filled eyes but seemed to understand. The hawk took to the air over him, ever the watchful guardian. Petros gently, with some effort, picked up the dog and carried him to his small rowboat, and together, he and his new companions moved out to the trawler.

Although it was somewhat of a challenge, Silvano Petros managed to get the dog aboard. His cat took one look at it and disappeared into one of his many hiding spots. Somehow — and in truth, Petros was amazed — the dog let him carry it into the hold, where he placed the creature on a rug in what served as the cabin. Even more remarkable was the damned hawk, who sat on the stern rail and chirped angrily while watching the affair, as if offering not-so-veiled threats.

Silvano was, of course, curious about the hawk and how it had arrived on the scene at just the right moment, and in truth, that was a story in itself. From the moment Cielo had been thrown free in the raging storm, life became a battle. As powerful as the bird was, the savage winds were simply too much, and the hawk was forced to partially fold his wings and simply sail toward the earth in something somewhere between a battered glide and a tumble. After an ungainly but successful landing, he took refuge in a hollow tree for the duration of the storm. But Cielo set out the following day, soaring upwards and outwards, searching along the river and the jungle on both sides, knowing intuitively that his lady had to be somewhere below in the morass of tree and vine and water. He flew by sensing more than searching, attuned to all the primal elements of perception that man had once been gifted with but had long since lost, having traded the greater senses of divination and premonition for physical gratification, blind ambition, and the primitive pleasures of the moment.

The dog had lost a lot of blood and was very weak. Silvano knew the whole thing was still a roll of the dice. But as the sun set and evening came on, the dog relaxed and accepted some water. It sighed then and stretched out, and closed its eyes, and the old Italian did something that he hadn't done seriously for a long time. He looked up and offered a simple prayer. "*Dios*, I know that he means little to me," he said, holding out his hands. "And not much more to you, I suppose. It is just a dog, *si*? But chu know, in truth, I suppose I wouldn't mind a companion like this." He shrugged. "Maybe you could save him, and I could take the credit, and we both win, eh?" Then he shook his head and huffed, "But that damn hawk! *Dios!* I'ne not so sure about that. And Carlos, my cat, won't be happy..." He let out another breath. "Okay, okay, maybe a package deal, huh?"

There was one other not-so-small motivation for Silvano regarding the dog. The Italian con man was in a bit of a crux at the moment. He had taken a huge chance — the chance of a lifetime — and the truth was, it was pretty much a "now or never" thing because he was getting too damned old and he had little or no place to turn for refuge — no family left and no real friends. He had a wife once but she left him, and he had no children (that he knew of) and no one to be there in his fading years. So he had seen an opportunity and he had taken it.

Petros had been working part-time as a cook at one of the diamond mine processing facilities in the jungle, where they dug out and processed diamonds and emeralds. They actually had an expert — a well-renowned "cutter" on-site, who did the final design cutting there. This way, the company airplane came into their strip and picked up finished products, rather than having to deal with more opportunity for theft and trickery somewhere else. Of course, the entire compound was guarded by a small army.

Somehow Silvano Petros had made the acquaintance of the primary cutter there — the man who shaped the stones in the most advantageous and visually remarkable fashion. For some reason, they had become friends — drinking buddies, you might say. Unfortunately, the cutter was a serious alcoholic at night. (Who wouldn't be after being locked in a room all day, staring at stones that had to be cut perfectly or your boss would take you out and shoot you?)

As it turned out, the cutter, a fellow named Santiago Chias, felt he really wasn't getting what he deserved for such a specialized job, so he started stealing diamonds. Well, *pieces* of diamonds might be more correct. He would cut a large diamond in such a fashion as to leave a couple of small but nice chips intact, and he would pocket one of them after a quick cutting. He had a tiny leather bag full of petite, precious stones that would allow him to live like a king and he was about to retire...

The only problem with his plan was the being seriously drunk part, and during that time, he mentioned in a very slurred fashion, before he passed out one night, his "special diamond cutting and saving," and the fact that he was about to retire. A wise man once said that alcohol can violate your standards quicker than you can lower them. Such was the case here.

One night, after Chias had passed out, Petros rifled the man's shack and found the small leather bag tied into the bedsprings. Petros shook his head. The man was remarkable with diamonds, but he couldn't hide an acorn from a blind squirrel. The old pirate didn't take them all, he only took about a half-dozen of the perfect stones — more than enough to last him a lifetime. He possessed an old, battered silver locket on a tarnished silver chain — his only possession from his mother — and he wore it around his neck always. He put the stones into the locket, which just barely held them all, and slipped its silver chain back around his neck.

The following day, Silvano Petros loaded what scant gear he had onto his trawler, said good-bye to his acquaintances, and sailed off downriver toward Caracas and the coast. There would be no more living like a pauper. Life was going to be good now.

The next day, he ran into the jaguar and the dog and the damned bird…

Oh well, it was what it was. The old pirate reached up and touched the pendant around his neck. He sighed and relaxed. Moving to his battered pantry, he cut a piece of meat from a clearly out-of-date haunch, then turned to his new companions. "We all go to sleep now," he whispered. "Tomorrow is another day, and Caracas won't come to us."

No one could have known, but during this time, there were a couple more scenarios of some import being written.

The gods, they like interesting, and they appreciate the hearts of kind fools, and they are clever how they make their entertainment…
— Rufus

CHAPTER SIX

Travis and Cody were sitting in Two Friends Restaurant in Key West, reading the latest reports of the huge storm off the coast of Venezuela. Apparently, there were places where the winds had reached hurricane strength. Travis contacted the authorities on both sides of the pond. There was no word on their friends. The Federal Aviation Administration had nothing — just an estimated time and location where contact was lost. The Venezuelan government had no news on a Grumman Goose landing at any airport. They did have a few seconds of communication with the pilot of a plane in the storm, none of which was good. The plane was lost, and to this point, an initial search had turned up nothing. The Venezuelan jungle was a big place.

Cody ran the fingers of one hand through his long blond hair and sighed. He looked at his friend. "You got a bag packed?"

Travis nodded. "Yep. Your plane fueled?"

Cody nodded. "Yep." He exhaled decisively. "I'll meet you at the airport FBO in an hour."

Richard Thomason, the newest director of the Smithsonian, had just received a fax from his team leader in South Florida. It seemed that the morning *Key West Citizen* had an article on the loss of a U.S. plane in Venezuela. Apparently, a number of the missing included several of the people who had given his organization such fits a little while back in the Southwest.

"What a shame," he muttered sarcastically. Thomason picked up the phone and dialed a series of numbers. When a voice on the other end answered, he briefly explained the loss of the aircraft and who was aboard. "Stay close to this, Simpson," he growled. "Let me know who lived and who died." There was a pause. "And I want to know what the living were doing down there and where they are now, you understand? Get on a plane, now!"

Bill Simpson straightened up and nodded, even though he was

on the phone. "Yes sir, you can count on it."

As it turned out, even a number of the living wanted to know what they were doing and where they were.

Meanwhile, in Key West...

Rinco Rodriguez (AKA "Animal Man") was also reading the morning paper. He was profoundly saddened that this particular plane was missing. No one knew it, but he had closely followed the exploits of the group affectionately called the Hole in the Coral Wall Gang. He often enjoyed a drink at Crazy Eddie's bar, and a couple of times, Key West's relatively famous "gang" had been there, celebrating, recounting, and enjoying the high that comes with rolling the dice and walking away in one piece.

Rodriguez understood that feeling fairly well. He was quite the gambler himself and no less gutsy in the occupations he had chosen previously — personal protection for the renowned and wealthy, military demolitions in the Middle East, and now, as sort of a hobby (because there sure as hell wasn't any money in it) defender of animals here and there. The difference being, he couldn't talk much about or take any credit for his present "moonlighting." Not that the credit mattered. But he missed raising a drink with friends who had done good and survived the day.

He had also shared this life with a couple of extraordinary animals (and boarded a guest on occasion) and had come to realize that, as with almost everything, integrity was the cornerstone of friendship. With animals, you almost inevitably got back more than you gave if you were willing to give. With humans...it was a roll of the dice.

Rinco had found a new message that caught his attention on the pool table blackboard at Sloppy Joe's. While knocking the balls around a little, he made mental notes on the message — a dog-fighting ring on Stock Island. There weren't many details (there never were), just an address and a time in an area that he knew had "gone Caribbean."

Key West, like many southern cities on the cusp of the Caribbean, had become its own worst enemy. Chaotic, barely controlled expansion and mindless greed inciting the need for cheap labor, and the proximity to the poorer islands of the Caribbean — primarily Haiti, which was a political and social car wreck at the best of times — were causing dramatic changes in the community's social infrastructure. Crime was soaring, poverty was expanding (hell, it was being imported), and along with all this came a huge increase in the basest of diversions — prostitution, gambling rings, illegal drugs, and one of the most sordid and depraved of all of man's entertainments, animal fighting contests.

Rodriguez shook his head and huffed out a bitter sigh. *Greed is a curse and it never leaves you better than you were before.* He finished the game with a clever bank shot on the eight, pulled the "fiver" off the rail, and nodded to his opponent, then racked his cue. He decided he'd have a look at this dogfight situation.

An hour later, after a challenging search, he found a battered series of "You Rent" storage facilities down a back road near the docks. There were a couple of large rentals at the end the size of a decent apartment, and in the adjacent parking lot were several cars — way too many for a storage rental gig. Rodriguez could see a big, burly-looking black guy standing at the doorway to the last "rental," smoking a cigarette — greasy ringlets of coarse black hair, a blunt nose with wide nostrils, and dark, angry eyes. There was light seeping out from the bottom of the vertical sliding door, and even from where he was, Rinco could hear a muffled, coarse roar coming from the other side. It rose and fell — the hoarse cries of gamblers, the snarls of enraged animals, and the cries of pain.

The ex-soldier parked his car a block away and came back around on foot to the entrance he's seen. He started toward the door but a big, chocolate-skinned man stepped out of the shadows in front of him.

"You got an invitation?" the guy asked, holding out a huge hand.

"Yeah, I do," replied the ex-soldier as he pulled a stun gun from his side and pressed it against the man's ribs. The guy was big, so Rodriguez held it against him for an extraordinarily long time, watching him "dance." (No, that wasn't true. The soldier held it against the trembling man, watching his eyes fill with shock and seeing him shiver in pain and terror because he was enjoying it.) He

58

wanted to do it to every god-damned person in that room — every one of those assholes who were in the process of reveling in the blood and the death of innocent, intelligent creatures for nothing more than the pleasure of watching it happen. They called it gambling, but it was nothing more than the exercise of a sickness that lived inside them. They weren't courageous enough themselves to fight someone on even terms and exorcise the demons that lived within them, and gambling at the dog track just didn't carry the visceral thrill they needed. No, this was how they got their jollies. Watching creatures murder each other for a fistful of dollars.

The ex-soldier stepped over the guard and entered the smoke-trellised, dimly lit room, which was fitted with a couple of rows of bleachers on two sides. In the center was a fifteen-foot, oblong ring with four-foot-high aluminum siding all the way around (to protect the onlookers). Above it all was a single, six-foot battery of fluorescent lights. Even as Rodriguez stood there, the pandemonium was rising to an ugly crescendo. One of the dogs in the ring (a huge Rottweiler with slavering, blood-splashed jaws) had pinned an exhausted and bloodied German shepherd to the floor and was tearing at its throat. Rodriguez couldn't believe what he was seeing. Standing there, the soldier's stomach turned. He'd seen his share of death but it usually came with some degree of purpose, even hope for something more or better. But this was just murder for the pleasure of speculation. There was no honor here, no sense of principle or pride. It was just death for dollars — paying for the privilege of witnessing homicide.

There was a final gurgling snarl that melted into a couple of harsh gasps, and then it was over. The cries and cheers faded down and away. All that was left were the cockcrows of a few winners, along with the bitter grumbling and the foul curses of the gamblers who had lost.

A tall black man in dirty cargo shorts and a sleeveless T-shirt pulled the body of the dead dog away and dragged it over to a pile of at least three other animals by the wall. He then moved the limping and bloodied survivor to a chicken-wire pen in the back. Rodriguez found himself trembling with anger. He wanted to pull his pistol and just start shooting... But the soldier checked himself, then did a quick recon. There was a mixed crowd, mostly Caribbean blacks but a few whites — some who looked like they had money and some who looked like they had found the money so they could exercise the ugliness that lived in their souls. The party was breaking up. A big islander (probably Jamaican or Bahamian, from the accent) had stepped forward to a microphone. Rinco had to look twice. The fellow effortlessly drew attention. The man was about five foot eight and built like a refrigerator — not unusual there, but he was an albino, and an extraordinary one at that. His skin was a light pink/cream color, and his curly afro was almost yellow, yet his features were still African — broad nose, flared nostrils, wide lips. But it was the eyes that stopped Rinco. They were a deep, hard green, like emeralds, and large. The whole image was somewhere between fascinating and unnerving.

The man was reminding the crowd that winners could collect their money from the betting window by the door, and this would happen again next week, same time, but he intimated that there was at least one other location.

Hmmm...

Everyone was sort of milling around at the moment, gulping down the remainder of their drinks and letting the adrenaline settle. Rinco decided to get out before anyone noticed the bouncer's body. He casually slid over to the door and slipped away.

The fresh air felt exceptionally good — even as humid as it was. The soldier exhaled, trying to expel the anger and shock. He needed to catch his breath. War was one thing — everyone knew the game and brutality was part of it. But this...this tore at something inside of him. Death for sport and a few bloody dollars.

———

While Travis and Cody were rising over the Straits of Florida, the challenges of life and death in Venezuela were heating up for the remaining members of the Hole in the Coral Wall Gang.

As soon as they had tumbled out of Eddie's Goose and into the storm that night, Tax had gotten a visual on his sister. She was a couple hundred yards to the west of him. But the trick was keeping her in sight with the billowing sheets of gray clouds and the wind ripping at him, jerking him around like a marionette managed by a drunk. He got one last look at Eddie's Goose as it buried itself in the clouds, moving downward way too fast...then he concentrated on keeping his sister in view. Storms oftentimes have stratums due to precipitation, wind, and temperatures. This one was no different. Both he and his sister had burst through the worst of the clouds and found themselves in a high-wind situation, but not much in the way of an overcast. Tax had more of a history with parachuting than Jing, having done some base-jumping on their home island of Barbados, and he was able to force his chute in her direction as they were both drawn toward the ground. The other advantage they had was exiting the plane first when it was closer to the coast. The terrain was not so much jungle and carried some agriculture and towns as well, and the land had been cleared in many places. Although the storm occluded everything to a degree, it wasn't completely dark yet, and Tax chased his sister toward the earth, working the old layman's parachute for all it was worth.

It should have been impossible. There were a dozen reasons why he should have lost her — the terrible winds and the thick clouds, the blinding rain — but he didn't. Jing went down in a hillside pineapple field about twenty miles from the coast. Tax came in three hundred yards east of his sister. The odds of that were just...well...let's just say there wasn't a track gambler in South America who would have taken a bet on that long horse.

But actually, it got better. They hit the ground about two hundred yards from a main road that would take them into a small agricultural hub called Caucagua, in the western highlands of Venezuela. Granted, Caucagua wasn't much of a "hub" by most standards. But it did have a couple of general stores, a market, two bars, a barbershop, an acceptable whorehouse, and a bank.

But once again, this is where those damned bored gods just couldn't leave well enough alone...

The body of the storm was passing. The winds had diminished and the rain had just about stopped. It was around seven o'clock. The best plan seemed to be to find some lodging in the distant town. It wasn't a pleasant journey, but a half hour later, they had made it into Caucagua (or so the sign said). Jing spotted what looked like a hotel on the main road in (and it was, albeit somewhat run down). The two of them looked like vagabonds — soaked and muddy, and exhausted, but the clerk forgave that when they said they were Americans. But Tax had lost his wallet in the commotion of falling out of airplanes and chasing Jing. It could be anywhere over about a twenty-mile radius. They booked a room with two beds, giving the clerk a very peripheral version of what had happened. Jing paid with her credit card. The clerk, of course, spoke in Spanish but Tax and Jing spoke Spanish well, with near-perfect inflection, having been born and raised in Barbados, just off the coast of Venezuela.

Once they were settled in and had cleaned themselves up as best they could, Jing found a number for the local Venezuelan Aviation Administration but the office was already closed. She tried what would be the area police station and was told they were too busy right now with local emergencies to be of any help. The fellow she spoke with said to come by the following day and they would take a report.

It looked like there was little they could do until morning, so they settled in and had drinks and a bite to eat at the hotel bar. Neither was really hungry. They were both terrified, not knowing what happened to their respective fathers. (And rightfully, they should have been...) Finally, the two vagabonds returned to their room, and with most of their clothes drying in the bathroom, they called it a night.

The following morning, Tax and his sister bought some clothes at a little shop next to the hotel. Tax, with his blondish hair slipping out of a natural straw Colombian cowboy-style hat, and clothed in white cotton *pantalones*, a T-shirt, and a cheap poncho, looked much like a native. Jing chose a T-shirt as well, and a pair of traditional American-style jeans. Then the two found a small cantina and had a little breakfast. They still weren't all that hungry but a cantina is a good place to get information. The waitress told them where to find the police station and the bank. They needed to meet with the local authorities as soon as possible, but realizing they were going to be in-country for a while, they also needed to get some money on a credit card and rent a car. And they needed to find their family. Daylight was burning.

The next stop now was the bank, which was right down the road. Then they'd rent a car and meet with the authorities.

The two of them should have remembered one of Rufus's

favorite sayings... *"Plans...hah! You be like monkeys dancing in da moonlight! You only get what you want when da gods got full bellies and be relaxin' in da shade. But if dey be bored, mon...plans be worthless as a turd in a coconut."*

The car rental thing with Jing went well. The bank...not so well.

The first thing they didn't know was that the daughter of the Minister of Finance for Venezuela had done what young people often do — she and a couple of her friends were going to a country spa in the middle of nowhere, near a little town called Caucagua. She was told it was too dangerous and she was not to go. But she did anyway. She had stopped by the bank in town for some money on her credit card.

It was a ten-minute stroll along the wooden boardwalk of not-so-beautiful downtown Caucagua to its only "lending and storage institution." The bank looked like something right out of the 1860's Midwest — a high, flat façade in front, with two large, curtained windows and an entrance between them. There were a couple of cars and a pickup out front, and a nondescript gray paneled van parked off to the side. Tax shrugged and opened the door, and things pretty much went downhill from there.

As he and Jing stepped through the door and moved over to an obviously anxious teller, Tax noticed that there seemed to be a bit of tension in the air. He suddenly realized it might have had something to do with the little guy by the teller (long black hair tied in a ponytail, dressed in white *pantalones* and an Aerosmith T-shirt) who, at that point, drew a pistol and began waving it in the air.

"Ariba! Ariba!" cried the fellow "Nobody gotta get hurt here, but you don' pay attention, I shoot your face off!" He raised his arms. *"Viva de Liberationists! Viva de Redistrabutionists!"* he shouted. "Take from the rich and give to the people!"

Tax might have argued that a good portion of that money in the banks was probably already the people's but this didn't seem like a good time.

The truth was, Tax and Jing had just stumbled into more than a simple bank robbery — they had suddenly become involved in the (at that moment) failing plans of an international money manipulation scheme involving a handful of investors in the U.S.

and a major company in Venezuela. And now, unfortunately for the manipulators, a testy little bandit.

It was a clever scheme. Yes, it was. But the best-laid plans of mice and men...

An American investment group had recently, very quietly, agreed to buy a large number of shares of a struggling but fairly sizeable Venezuelan manufacturing company. They would, however, receive considerably more shares than what were ostensibly shown on the contract, and they would make additional money on the manipulation of the stock as well. Their responsibility in the scheme was to send the Venezuelan company owners some cash — American dollars, lots of American dollars — for the shares they purchased. Venezuela was suffering with the onset of a serious devaluation of their dollar, the bolivar, at this time and it was to get worse. Nobody wanted Venezuelan dollars. Not even the Venezuelans. American dollars were like gold there.

This in-country corporation, based out of Caracas, would, in turn, invest three-quarters of the American money into their own company — abruptly driving up their "board value" — and steal the other quarter (all of which was in wonderfully viable American dollars). The immediate upward movement of the Venezuelan company on the international stock exchange would drive up the shares, creating a positive run on the stock and allowing the "recent investors" in America to make serious money as well. Everyone would win — the Venezuelan company would become more solvent again for a little while, the owners would pocket some American "side money," and the U.S. investors would dump the Venezuelan group's shares while "at peak" before the artificially manipulated prices began to fall.

The only thing that made the plan a little precarious was the transfer of the huge amount of cash to make it work — a hundred thousand American dollars. No one wanted to show the transfer and have to explain where the money came from and why, and most of all, with the huge inflation of Venezuelan money (a hundred American dollars being worth about a zillion Venezuelan bolivars), the only way to do this was to have a "special courier" carry the hundred grand from the U.S. to a small, innocuous bank somewhere in Venezuela — where the Venezuelan conspirators could simply drop by and pick up a couple of suitcases packed with U.S. hundred-dollar bills. (Again, most of which they would invest in their own company to drive up stock ratings, and a small part of which they would spend on expensive rum and beautiful whores.)

It was really pretty simple, and this whole thing would have worked just fine but for the careless words of a couple of Venezuelan executives during a three-martini lunch, and a janitor with exceptional ears and a larcenous heart who just happened to be friends with a small but ballsy bandit named Tito Ro.

When he heard about it from the janitor, Tito Ro laughed out loud. If it was true...*if*...it was just too good to be true. To steal the money from the very people who were robbing the citizens of Venezuela — the politicians and banking gangsters — and then find a way to give "most of it" back to the people in some gloriously extroverted fashion. *Caramba! Muy bien!*

The irony was, Tito Ro had always dreamed of making one magnificent gesture for which he would be remembered. There was a tower at the top of the Metropolitan Cathedral of Saint Anne in the center of Caracas, on a hillside above the entire city. If the wind was blowing right, it would carry paper money across the city! The real problem was the drastically devaluated Venezuelan money. An entire suitcase of the country's highest denomination wouldn't be worth more than a couple hundred American.

But...if everything his janitor buddy had told him was true, a hundred thousand American in fifties and hundreds would be in the Bank of Caucagua on Wednesday morning. It would be picked up Thursday morning. It was a small window but it was enough.

Now, back at the bank...

As the small robber shouted revolutionary slogans, a big fellow (long black hair, five-day stubble, a few teeth...) on the other side of the room suddenly produced a sawed-off, double-barreled shotgun from under his coat. On the other side of the room, there was a dark-haired, middle-aged woman in a red-flowered mumu just a few feet from the little guy, who was now confidently holding her pistol, covering everyone.

"Viva la revolucion!" shouted the little guy again as he moved

over to the bank president's desk and dragged him back to the vault. A moment later, it swung open and the bandit was dragging out the couple of satchels of cash that had been destined for the unscrupulous Venezuelan company executives.

Tax looked at Jing, who recognized immediately that it was better to be on the team with the guns at this moment.

"Viva la revolucion!" they shouted.

The few customers in the bank were very close to freaking out. Tax wasn't at all sure where all this was going, but after studying the "bandits," who didn't seem all that dangerous, he figured there was a real good chance of everybody surviving and he and Jing walking away.

Just when you think you've got it figured out...

Tax and his sister were standing by a door that appeared to lead to the interior of the bank. Suddenly, it swung open and a Venezuelan soldier stepped out with a short-barreled, Uzi-type machine gun cradled in his arms. His eyes were hard and hot; there wasn't a lot of negotiation in them anywhere. He was raising the weapon.

Tax was a quick study. This was about to become a blood bath and there was a fair chance no one would walk out. The young man did the most logical thing — maybe not the most legal thing, but the most logical. Before the soldier could bring the gun up, Tax stepped in and chopped him on the neck. A short staccato of rounds from the guard's weapon dug into the wooden floor and he dropped like he'd been pole-axed. Tax quickly kicked away the machinegun. The bandits in the room snapped around like meerkats.

The little guy nodded in appreciation. *"Bueno, amigo,"* he muttered with a smile. *"Bueno..."*

"Well, that really tears it, Sundance," Jing said under her breath.

There was one other person in the room who had tucked herself into a corner and was pretending she was part of the wood paneling — a young girl, obviously very frightened. There were tears in her eyes and she was heaving in breaths. The girl was relatively well dressed — not a peasant. She looked at Tax. Their eyes met and locked for a moment, and something electric and strange passed between them. Tax smiled and blew her a kiss to assure her that she was safe.

"Esta bien, chiquita," he whispered. *"Esta bien…"*

"Let's go! *Ariba! Ariba!"* shouted the little guy with the pistol and the cash satchels, breaking the spell. *"Viva la revolucion!"*

"Viva la revolucion!" cried the others.

About that time, the big grimy fellow stepped over, headed for the young, very frightened girl. It looked like maybe he'd decided to take a memento of the experience.

Tax quickly moved in between them, eyes defiant, body language changing to something that said he'd done this before. "Leave her," he growled in Spanish. "You want her, you have to come through me."

And the heat in his eyes was enough to make the man back off. The guy exhaled, shrugged like it didn't matter, and turned away. The girl stared at Tax for a moment and their eyes held briefly. He smiled. *"Esta bien, chiquita,"* he whispered again. *"Estas seguro…*You're safe." Then he broke contact. But it didn't matter. Her heart had just been stolen.

Tax quickly turned to one of the tellers close to him. "We're not bandits," he stuttered in Spanish. "You have to understand, we're not —"

But the look on the terrified teller's face (as she jammed the alarm button under the counter with one hand) said none of that was computing. He and his sister were, without doubt, being listed on the bandits' team, and he had heard too many horror stories about Americans caught in bad situations south of the border.

The young man looked at Jing, who was also a quick study.

"Viva la revolucion," she muttered with a smile, and in the next two minutes the bandit revolutionists, including Tax and Jing, were headed out the door.

At the last moment, the man with the long black hair swung around at the doorway, and with a smile and a wave shouted, *"Via con Dios, amigos e amigas!"*

It was all really strange. Way out of whack. It all seemed like a hashish dream.

When they got outside, next to an old panel van that had a dripping paintbrush and a house painted on its side, Tax had planned on grabbing his sister and making a dash. They had things they needed to do. They had friends and family lost somewhere out there, and they didn't have time for weird side roads. But before he could get his sister's attention and maybe get away, the small bandit turned, forcefully grabbed Tax by the arm, and whispered, "Did you bring the guns?"

Tax glanced at his sister. She shrugged helplessly.

"No, no guns…"

The little bandito stared at them incredulously. "I ask for men and guns and Pedro sends me one pale gringo and a gringa?"

Tax looked at his sister again. They were into this act now and there was nowhere to go without possibly getting shot. He turned back to the bandit. "Yeah, yeah, should have been more, but you know how the bandit business is. It has its ups and downs. They caught Pedro and Julio."

The little bandit tilted his head questioningly. "Pedro? Julio?" He exhaled heavily and held up a hand. "Okay, okay, never mind. Get in! Get in!" He waved at the van.

Tax and Jing could have said no…but they had just robbed a bank.

The last thing Tax saw as they started to drive away was the pretty young lady he had defended, standing in the doorway of the bank, staring at him. He smiled and blew her a kiss. There was a strange connection there that he didn't understand. But there wasn't time for that today, and this wasn't the place.

They drove at a righteous clip for about fifteen minutes, twisting into the mountains, headed for a little hideout the group had. Everyone was still just a little high from the robbery and the bottle of tequila that was being passed around. Introductions were made. The crazy little honcho who was driving was Tito Ro. The woman was Angela, the big guy with the bad teeth was Rodriguez. Tax decided to be a "Gilligan" and Jing was now "Mary Ann." (Those were the first names that came to mind — they seemed…good… given the situation.)

After they were well underway, Tito looked over his shoulder at Tax. He spoke in English. "You be *Americanos,* no?"

Tax glanced at Jing (*no point in lying*). "Yeah, *correcto,* but we were raised in Barbados." He took a chance and asked, "Well, Tito, is this your regular job or do you only do this on the weekends? And how's this working out, you know, after expenses?"

Tito smiled. "I'm a painter — house painter by profession," he said over his shoulder in relatively good English. "We only rob banks on weekends." He threw up a hand and the van slipped off onto the side of the road slightly. "*Si, si,* we do robbin', *si,* but we give da money to da revolution — to da people! Dat be, how you say, our job description." He straightened up and got serious. "Chu know how many children go to bed without any food tonight? Many go to bed without beds! Twenty percent of da people in Venezuela take eighty percent of da money while the other eighty percent starve. Our government now got what dey call 'austerity measures' — which means da people in da palaces keep da money and da people in da streets starve. You complain, dey chut chu."

"Chut chu?"

"Yeah, yeah, you know…" He held up a hand in the shape of a gun, putting a forefinger to his head. "Bang, bang…you know, and tomorrow your wife be a widow." He exhaled hard, determined, and got that cocky half-smile again. "But tomorrow, dis money gonna get dropped from da top of the tower of de Metropolitan Cathedral of Saint Anne in the center of Caracas — and if the wind is right, it blow all dose hundred-dollar bills across de city!"

He held out his hands and laughed, those dark brown, BB eyes shining with anticipation and delight. "Dis will be our third liberation of *dolares* from de Venezuelan government — our third re-distribution of Venezuela's wealth."

"You don't keep any for yourselves?" Tax asked cautiously.

"Only enough for gas and tequila. Dis not about us. Dis about makin' the world see da truth about our country…and feeding people."

He paused. And for the first time, Tax saw the man in a different light. He was crazy for sure…but it was a good crazy.

"You guys are real-life Robin Hoods," Jing muttered, reluctantly impressed.

The fellow nodded. "Yeah, I hear dat name before — some English bandito, *si*?" He smiled. "Oohhh, *chiquita*, I like to have a drink with him an' tell some stories…"

Tax shook his head. "Nah, he's gone now. It's been a while…"

Tito held up a finger. "But da people still remember him." He paused and his eyes went serious for a moment, and he waved a forefinger. "If your story gets written down, you never really die..." His face became pensive, his eyes distant. "Dat's important, gringo. To be remembered. Dat's important..." Our little bandit exhaled again heavily. "But right now we got to hide de money. Everybody gonna be lookin' for us, and we don' wanna be caught with the *dolares*."

"You got a place?" Jing asked cautiously. "To hide it..."

Tito nodded. "We go dere now..."

Jing looked at her brother and shrugged. "In for a penny, in for a pound," she said under her breath. "Besides, we just robbed a bank..."

An hour later, they were on the outer edges of Caracas, just before where the city started. Tito had dropped off the others of his team at a couple of locations after giving them each a handful of dollars for "running and hiding money," as he called it. Now it was just Jing, Tax, and Tito. The ruins of what must have been a mansion of sorts stood in front of them, mostly destroyed by fire and time. There was, however, enough roof left on one side to protect what might have been a study or a living room. Tito parked and they exited the van cautiously.

Tito led everyone to a corner of the ruins. He pushed back a couple of burned roof timbers, then looked up. "Many years ago, I help paint this place." He smiled. "And I remember something..."

He reached down and found a metal ring. He pulled and the cellar door came up out of the ashes.

With some degree of trepidation, Tax and Jing followed their new acquaintance down the stairs. Tito lit a couple of oil lanterns. It was a fairly large room — nicely furnished and largely untouched by the fire that had destroyed the house. There were two couches and a couple of mattresses, a kitchen table, and there was an impressive wine rack with bottles still intact.

Well, quite a few of the bottles were missing, but hey...

There was a sink and hand pump for water that had obviously been installed by Tito. "Welcome to my home," said the little man as he set the bags of money on the table — easily a small fortune. *"Mi casa es su casa..."* He sighed. "I must go back out. There are people who will need to know about the money release from the tower of the cathedral tomorrow — my circle..."

Tax and Jing nodded in understanding.

"Do you need us?" Tax asked hesitantly. He didn't want to become involved in this any more than they already were, and he didn't want to risk his sister.

The house painter/bank robber waved him off. "*No es necessarrio, amigo.* This is my job, now."

CHAPTER SEVEN

During the early part of the evening, Tax was wandering about, feeling somewhat imprisoned, when he came to a manila folder on the kitchen table. He had nothing to lose and he was bored, so he opened it. Inside, he discovered a brief but remarkably well-written account of Tito's involvement in the efforts to free Venezuela's people from the oppression of a disconnected upper class and the country's brutal military junta, beginning with the man's early efforts, after his parents died, to his remarkable five-year history as a revolutionist for a free and prosperous Venezuela. Tax was surprised and touched by the man's width and breadth of knowledge and emotion, and simple courage. When he finished reading, Tax set down the papers and exhaled softly. "If your story gets written down, you never really die..." he whispered to himself.

They waited through the night and into the morning, but Tito never came back. Finally, Tax decided to hitchhike into Caracas for some supplies and a paper. An hour later, he returned.

Jing took one look at him and her shoulders fell. "What happened?" she whispered.

Her brother shook his head sadly and set the newspaper on the table. "The police raided a house of insurgents last night." He sighed. "There was a gunfight. They killed them all and apparently broke up a plan to distribute a hoard of stolen money to the Venezuelan populace. Evidently, they didn't learn how this was going to be done, only that this was the intention. They are still looking for the money from the bank robbery yesterday."

Tax exhaled angrily, and when he looked up at his sister, there was a hard look of determination in those hazel eyes. "They killed Tito but I'm not going to let them kill his last dream."

"Tax," Jing said softly, "it's not your fight...not our windmill..."

The young man sighed. "C'mon," he said. "We've got some shopping to do. I need a base-jumping parachute. And a wide-mouthed hiking pack."

It didn't take much for Jing to realize what was happening.

"Tax," she said evenly, trying to keep control of the situation. "You don't have to... You'll risk everything — your freedom, maybe your life. They can kill you."

Her brother looked at her. "Tito deserved more than he got. I read about him last night. He was a silent hero — the kind you read about in novels." Tax got that soft smile of his, then it faded into determination and he quoted his father. "Sometimes a man's got to do what a man's got to do. There just ain't no getting around it. You've just got to take it to the limit —"

"One more time..." added Jing, almost sadly.

Like Tax said as they hitchhiked into the city with a huge bag of stolen money, "Today, at least one dream is going to come true..."

It really was insane. Worse, it was stupidly dangerous, but there was something inside the young man that he just couldn't let go of. He had to try. But there was no point in standing on the parapets of the Metropolitan Cathedral of Saint Anne in the center of Caracas and tossing out money as Tito had planned. That was suicide. There was no escape, and the police would most likely have him before he finished his task. No, he had a plan. Maybe he could accomplish what Tito wanted and still get away.

Once they were in the city, they rented a car again. Tax remembered where the base-jumping shop was from their last visit to Caracas during the Incredible Key-West-Caribbean Race (when they had jumped off perfectly good cliffs to see who would wait the longest to "pull the cord"). There he found exactly what he was looking for — a simple base-jumping parachute that was a "quick-open," highly maneuverable design, without the sleeves for legs and arms.

Then they found a department store and bought a wide-mouthed, canvas backpack and an extra-extra-large canvas windbreaker to cover everything from curious eyes. They then found a gas station where Tax used the restroom briefly. There he donned the base-jumping parachute, then slipped on the backpack backward, on his front rather than on his back. He stuffed all the money into the pack (the old bandit had stolen a lot of money, and when all was said and done, Tax could barely get all the hundred-dollar bills into it), so during his descent, he could hastily reach in and pull out hundreds of bills at a time. Then he donned the big windbreaker. The whole thing — their plan — was a huge pain in the ass, but it was the only way for Tax to have a chance to distribute the money and still maybe evade the authorities. (Old Tito hadn't planned a getaway — he was just going to throw the money off the top of the church and hope to get lost in the crowd that would have inevitably developed.)

It wasn't hard to find the Metropolitan Cathedral of Saint Anne. It sat on a high piece of hillside at the northern end of the city. With its tall tower and the prevailing winds, it was the perfect place for a base-jump over the city of Caracas. In particular, and as the gods would have it, outside the circle of businesses that surrounded it were large *barrios* where the poor lived, squeezing out their day-to-day existence.

The plan was to leap from the tower and aim the flight southeast, which would carry Tax across a good portion of the slums of Caracas, during which time he would empty his backpack and the brisk wind would do the rest. From there, it was a fairly straight shot into the Botanical Gardens of Caracas, where his sister would be waiting with the car. The gardens had a few flat areas and some green lawns for a possible landing. It was a roll of the dice at best, dangerous as hell, and Tax had about a fifty percent chance of ending up in jail by the end of the day, but there was no stopping him. He was going to fulfill the old bandit's last wish.

Two hours later, Tax and Jing were standing in front of the cathedral. Tax looked like a rather obese man but he didn't draw much attention. The two adventurers stared at each other and nodded, then turned and entered the cathedral to climb the long stairway up to the pinnacle — the observation tower. The tower was nearly two hundred feet above the ground, and given the high location of the building to begin with, they were practically touching the clouds.

As they stood on the parapet, a mated pair of black-collared hawks circled lazily above them in the wind currents. Tax turned and saw the look in his sister's eyes — the pain and the loss. He pulled Jing to him and held her tight for a moment, letting the pain of uncertainty pass. Then he pulled back and stared at his sister, his eyes carrying the excitement burning in his breast.

Jing gazed at him, half angry, half terrified for the brother she truly loved. "You know you're freaking crazy, don't you?"

He smiled. "You're just figuring that out?"

"Ooohh no, I've known for some time," she said with a sad smile of her own.

"I gotta go now," Tax said quietly.

Jing stared at him for a moment, as if she was trying to…remember him. She touched her brother's cheek gently, then reluctantly let the hand slide away. "Take it to the limit…" she whispered. "One more time…"

Tax turned, and to the amazement and surprise of the few tourists around them, he ripped off his huge jacket, exposing the backpack of money against his chest and stomach, and the parachute at his back, then he climbed up on the parapet and with one final look at his sister, he was gone — over the side and into the wind.

The plan for distributing the money went great. As soon as he was into a freefall, the wind pulling at him like a needy lover, Tax pulled his cord and the chute billowed out, offering that satisfying snap as it reached full-open, carrying him away from the cathedral and taking him toward the barrios and the people who needed his gifts. Once he stabilized, he ripped open the backpack and began grabbing handfuls of money and tossing them out, while periodically using alternate hands to keep the chute on course. (They had already removed the paper bands on the stacks of hundreds to aid in a broad distribution.)

It was truly *manna* from heaven. Soon a few people below were watching the crazy person throwing out paper. It took a while for the implications to catch on…

An old woman sat on her battered porch, smoking a poorly wrapped *cigarillo*. She was watching some crazy man in the sky above sail by and toss out squares of paper by the handfuls. "Mama" was old. She had seen a lot of stupid things and wasn't overly impressed. She took another puff of her *cigarillo* and eased out a gray cloud. But as the man passed by a few hundred feet above her, a hundred-dollar bill floated down and landed at her feet. She stared at it, then took another look at the skyman. Then she picked up the bill. Several others were floating down now, landing in the street, on parked cars, in alleyways, and on rooftops. She studied it, felt the texture, then her eyes went wide.

"Dios! Mi Dios!" she muttered with surprise and unbridled amazement. In the next second she was scrambling around in the alley like a young girl, clutching a fistful of dollars and chasing after the angel from Heaven.

Down the street, a taxi driver sat on the hood of his car, taking an early lunch. A hundred-dollar bill drifted down leisurely and landed on the hood next to him. He picked it up and stared at it incredulously. He could hear people now...some were yelling, some seemed to be crying and praying at the same time. Suddenly, the air was filled with floating bills. He looked up at what must be some crazy person flying in the sky in one of those parachute things and throwing out what appeared to be...money! In the next instant, he dropped his sandwich and was scrambling about with the rest of his neighbors.

Of course, the path that Tax took caused a good deal of havoc. Traffic jammed in places as people stumbled out of their vehicles, chasing the wind-blown hundreds. Sidewalk restaurants emptied, domino games came to a screeching halt, and even the police (who were poorly paid to begin with) became chasers of instant fortune. It was truly a case of blessed pandemonium for the needy and the undeserved.

But who's to say who is deserved and who is not, eh? God doesn't differentiate when it comes to luck. And that's what this was all about.

Speaking of timing and luck, there was one unique gift from the gods...

Travis and Cody had come back to Caracas to meet with Venezuela's aviation administration again for another report. They were having coffee at a small street-side café when the commotion broke out. Everyone had started calling out and pointing upwards. There, about three hundred feet above them, floated a man in a base-jump parachute, who was throwing money into the air by the fistfuls.

Cody squinted for a moment and brought a hand up over his eyes. He smiled. "Son of a bitch!" he whispered incredulously.

"Son...of...a...bitch! That boy is really learning how to make an entrance."

Travis was looking up now as well. He too had a broad grin painted on his face. "Like father like son," he said softly. He sighed. "Okay, let's chase him down. Something tells me this is going to get worse before it gets better."

That night, poor families across the city ate well. Children had all they wanted and no one went to bed hungry. Loans were repaid, rent was paid, deals were made, restaurants were packed, and some parents, for the first time in a long time, went to bed free of worry and fear.

It was a good damned thing — a miracle, everyone said...

However, it didn't work out so well for the two miracle workers. The landing for Tax, in the botanical gardens, worked well. The rest of the plan, not so much. The police picked up on what Tax was planning on doing about halfway through his distribution, and they were waiting for him when he finally hit the ground. He was immediately arrested as Jing watched helplessly from the street.

Tax would have probably been screwed to the wall, becoming a resident of Venezuela's prison system for years to come, but for one young girl who happened to see the headlines in the paper the next day — headlines that carried a photo of Tax in the arms of two policemen. The girl just happened to be the daughter of the Minister of Finance in Venezuela. She was also the young lady Tax had rescued from the ugly bank robber back in the little town of Caucagua.

She immediately arranged for a conversation with Dad.

"You save my daughter from dis man, she say. Dis barbarian robber in da bank." The Venezuelan Minister of Finance exhaled heavily, staring at Tax. "Now she is taken with you! Ha! I don' care if she thinks you are the most handsome man in the world." He shook a finger. "I do not think you are the most handsome man in the world. *Comprende?*"

"Yes sir," said Tax, who was standing in front of the minister, still in handcuffs. "Actually I'm relieved you don't think I'm handsome...given the circumstances..."

The minister skewered him with a stare, then huffed. "She has, all of a sudden, become a beautiful woman. Everyone wants to take her home."

Tax brought his hands up. "Not me, sir — no, not me."

"Why?" yelled the minister. "Why? She is not good enough for you, *gringo?* She is not beautiful enough?"

"Oh, no sir! I mean, yes sir! I'd take her home in a heartbeat," Tax babbled.

"Not without my permission, you wouldn't," cried the minister. "You would find yourself tied to a railroad track and missing parts you wish you still had!"

"Yes, sir. I mean...no, sir," said Tax. "She's wonderful and I'll take her if you want me to."

"I don' want you to!" cried the minister, slapping his hand on his desk. "You touch my daughter, I kill you twice!" He spat on the floor. "You make fools of us, throwing stolen American money across the city! And now, I must let you go or my daughter will never speak to me again. Worse yet, to save face, we are forced to announce that you were part of a government plan to gift the people." He threw up his hands. "That all this throwing of money away to peasants was our idea! Otherwise, we all look like impossible fools!"

"Well, it stands to reason that you can't very well arrest me for something you decided to do, right?" replied Tax cautiously.

The minister looked up at the young man. "An' how is it you become a bank robber in less than twenty-four hours in this country, huh? Huh?"

Tax shook his head. "Sir, we were never bank robbers. My sister and I came to the bank to get some money on our credit cards and got caught up in the robbery. The bandits thought we were part of their team, and at the time we thought it best not to disappoint them."

"Hmmm," growled the minister. "I think I could torture you for a day or two before I let you go, just to make sure..."

Tax shrugged. "That would disappoint your daughter, I bet."

The man stared holes through Tax for a moment, his Hispanic complexion turning a nice color of red. "You get out of here now, *gringo.* You get out of my city. You get out of my country. *Comprende?"*

"Yes sir. I do. I do indeed," the young man replied.

Later that day, when Tax finally found himself leaving the Venezuelan National Police compound in Caracas, he wasn't quite sure what to expect. He was extraordinarily pleased to see Jing waiting for him, and even more pleased when he saw Cody and Travis standing next to her.

"Son of a bitch!" he whispered with a smile. "Son of a bitch!"

Travis just shook his head and growled, "You've got a lot of your old man in you...always pushing the damned envelope." The big man huffed out a breath. "We need to get out of this city before you conjure up something else...stupid. We've got to find the rest of the team."

"You're right," said Tax, "but there's one last thing I have to do."

Actually, there were two things. First, Tax had Travis take everyone back to Tito's hideout under the burned-out mansion. There he picked up the copy of the old revolutionary's brief story. From there, they drove to the primary newspaper in the city — *El Universal.* Tax grabbed his package and got out of their car, then turned to his friends. "I'll be back in just a few minutes."

The editor of *El Universal* was a big, rotund man with a balding head and a fat, black mustache. He leaned back in his chair and his dark eyes became both cautious and curious when Tax mentioned Tito. Tax tossed him Tito's short story as a freedom fighter/ revolutionary/bank robber in Venezuela. It was only a handful of pages. Tito was a man of action, not so much of words. But it was a remarkably adroit description of the times and the struggle of the country, and it was quite well written for a bandit.

Tax explained that he would like the story printed in an upcoming paper — as soon as possible. The American would have been thrown out on his ear normally, but the editor recognized him from the article they'd just done about the money falling from the sky. So he took the time to look at it.

But in the end, it didn't fly. "I don' think so," said the editor cautiously. "It's the story of a bandit. Venezuela has lots of bandits, and this one was particularly not popular with the government." He sighed. "No point in jabbing the jaguar. *Comprende?*" He shrugged. "No... Sorry, *gringo*. No can do."

Tax took out an envelope and tossed it on the desk. Inside was a thousand dollars, American. "What about now?"

The editor glanced around, then opened the envelope cautiously, without picking it up, and did a quick count with his fingers. He looked up and smiled for the first time. "Would the morning edition tomorrow be okay?"

Tax moved closer but there was something about him that changed. He became instantly hard — purely dangerous. "I want it proofed, but I want the story printed like it is. If it's not, I'll come back for you." He leaned in even closer. "You are way too easy to find, and way too fat to run..."

The editor lost all his arrogance looking into those hazel eyes. "No *problemo, amigo...no problemo*...tomorrow morning."

The American nodded, then the smallest of sad smiles touched Tax's lips. "You see, *amigo,* if your story gets written down, you never really die..."

Children most often become their parents, despite their efforts to the contrary.

CHAPTER EIGHT

While Tax and Jing were playing catch-up with Travis and Cody, they learned the bad news — still no solid information on the lost plane and Eddie, and no info at all on their parents or their feathered and furred companions.

"The contacts we've spoken with say a couple of the villages on the Orinoco reported hearing a plane during the storm, close...then not hearing it anymore," Cody explained. He sighed. "So I guess we've got somewhere to start. But it's a big river."

He paused and Travis took over. "We've offered a reward for information, and I also found an FBO who would rent us a 182 Cessna on floats. This way, if we see something, we can act. We're headed out today — going to run along the high ground by a few of the rivers." He drew a breath and said the words they all had hidden from themselves. "I have to know, one way or the other..."

Tax and Jing nodded gratefully.

Jing looked at them all, her face set with determination. "While I breathe, I hope," she whispered harshly. And in the back of her mind, she hated herself for also being so concerned for her hawk — her companion who had proven to be beyond remarkable in their short relationship and had disappeared in the storm.

At this point, hope was all anyone had, including Will and me, as we continued to paddle along the muddy river. There was, sure as hell, no pulling in and taking a break on dry land. I was certain that one or both of us would end up as a snack. All we could do was take turns sleeping and paddling, and judiciously using what little food and water we had managed to grab as we fled the village.

The bad news in all this was the large canoe of jungle natives that had suddenly appeared and was following us, slowly closing in. There were probably a half-dozen men, all armed with bows, spears, and machetes.

"Hmmm," muttered Will. "Probably not good."

"Maybe they want to help us," I offered. "You know, they could have read something in the morning paper — or maybe they heard it on the drums."

"Or maybe their stew was just too watery last night," my friend said. "Not enough meat…"

Instinctively, we began to increase our strokes. So did the natives.

It swiftly became a race to nowhere and we were losing. Suddenly, an arrow hammered into the rear of the canoe, behind Will. That immediately increased our incentive. The big guy in the front of the boat behind us — dark-reddish skin, long black hair, holding a spear — yelled at us. Something between Spanish and the local native dialect. I didn't understand and I wasn't waiting for a language lesson. Another arrow thunked into the canoe next to the first one.

The big guy in the bow of his canoe stood up and yelled again, in English this time. "Hey! White idiots! Stop boat now!"

That got our attention.

A half hour later, we were beaching our boats at a large village downstream. Apparently, this group was closer to the coast and civilization, and was more advanced than our groupie lady friends upriver. It was explained to us that this village had a hand/solar-powered VHF radio on which they had heard about the missing plane and the reward that Cody and Travis had offered.

"When it comes to death and money, word travels fast," observed Will.

It didn't matter to us how it had happened. Will and I had been rescued. We were heading back to civilization.

The natives in the village used their VHF to contact the authorities in Caracas. Those authorities got a message to Cody and Travis. Our friends were on their way in their rented 182 floatplane to pick us up. That was the good news. The shaky news was, we learned that someone had just called in a report of finding a crashed aircraft deep in the mountain jungle. The remains of what looked like a large twin-engine, just off one of the dozens of rivers in this part of Venezuela, but deeper into the interior.

By nightfall, we were back in Caracas at a hotel — with hot showers, clean sheets, and hamburgers, French fries, and cold beer.

(I'd had all the fire-roasted animals and lizards I could handle for a while.) Tomorrow morning, we'd head out over the jungle to the site of the wreckage near the river. The only hurry was on our part. If Eddie was there, in that plane, he didn't need any help…

And through it all, along this whole adventure, it kept coming back to me in waves… Shadow, my boy… Where was he? He had to be okay. He *had* to be. I couldn't entertain the alternative. I just couldn't. I had watched him splash into the river that night…but how in God's name do you find a dog in a thousand square miles of jungle?

Then there was Jing's hawk, Cielo. What had happened to him? And our friend — our dear old friend, Crazy Eddie. There was a part of me that was terrified about finding that airplane.

The most painful farewells are the ones that are never said…

———————————

Silvano Petros, river pirate/trader-cum-recent diamond thief, cruised leisurely with the current for the next few days, heading for the coast and a small port city just outside Caracas. (The big cities had too many authorities, and some of them knew his name…) He was rather enjoying himself. The dog he had saved was doing well — remarkably well. The vein had closed nicely and the patch of flesh and fur that had been torn out by the big cat had "taken" to the old flesh. The remarkable dog that he had saved from the jaguar was healing, and was actually up on his feet a little.

The hawk was another matter. The bird scared the crap out of the old bandit. It was obviously attached to the dog somehow, and it hardly left its companion other than to catch a fish. Even then, it brought the fish back and ate it on the stern of the boat.

Petros shook his head, running the crooked fingers of one hand through his long, graying hair. He had never seen anything like it. It was like one of those sappy movies at the cinema — no one believes them but they like them. The whole thing struck a place inside him not often examined — a cave of hidden truths, the good and the bad that was Silvano Petros — and he was reminded of that fleeting, rarely visited issue called integrity. It wasn't that he didn't believe in honor, he just didn't practice it much.

He slid his hand down almost unconsciously to the silver locket on the tarnished chain around his neck, reminding himself of the Mother of Hope Mission on the coast, at the town of Maiquetia, and a promise he'd made. *Hmmm...*

Petros wasn't exactly devoid of virtue but he possessed what might be called "selective integrity." Most of the time, whatever it was he was doing wasn't important enough to him to require honor, but there were a couple of things that mattered in the old scoundrel's life. An occasional kindness bestowed and kindness received were paramount because, like diamonds, they were bright and rare. He touched the locket again. It was almost a caress. Yes, he would live up to his promise from so many years ago. Probably...if he could.

But he would keep a few stones for himself. He deserved it... Besides, *a thief who steals from a thief is pardoned for a hundred years* — or so it was said...

Speaking of shiny stones...

At the diamond mine camp upriver, where Silvano Petros had stolen his small fortune, there was a very unhappy diamond cutter. Enraged might be a better term. BB-spitting, crazy insane would work too. It turned out the Santiago Chias figured out what had happened. Actually, it didn't take much figuring. Chias was an arrogant, vengeful person at the best of times. Having someone steal some of his diamonds that he had worked so hard to steal really blew out all his plugs. He was too old to chase this bastard robber down by himself, so he hired two very ugly souls to help him run this rabbit to ground. It didn't take much intellect to figure out that Silvano Petros was going to make a run downriver to the coast, probably to Caracas. Several places in the city would buy his diamonds, no questions asked. A call was made and an older model, mechanically beefed-up Cessna172 floatplane arrived later that day with two men devoid of conscience. Santiago Chias was sparing no expenses. This wasn't just about money now. This was about revenge.

They would set out the following morning. That old wreck of a boat that Petros had wasn't anywhere near civilization yet. They'd catch him easily, and the crocodiles would love what they left.

By first light, my friends and I were at the airport in Caracas, doing a careful preflight and loading into our rented Cessna 182 floatplane.

Deep in the jungle, along a nameless river, Santiago Chias and his two henchmen were doing the same — preflighting their airplane and checking their weapons.

The sun had cleared the horizon and was painting the verdant tapestry of jungle and field a soft yellow as we lifted off. I sat at the left seat of the 182 — I owned a floatplane just like this one, so I was the most qualified to pilot it. We had some rough GPS coordinates and supposedly there was a river nearby that would provide access for a landing. It was, indeed, deeper into the interior than most of the search parties had been looking, and as we wound along the river, headed south, there was a yin and yang of anticipation. It would indeed be good if this was our friend's plane. We would have a point of reference for search parties, and clues to what had happened to Eddie…and, at worst, perhaps some closure for us all. But the truth was, once you get down into that jungle (thousands of miles of "heavy green," all of which connects to the thousands of miles of jungle in Brazil), it all just looks the same. You become mesmerized by the endless, green-and-brown blanket, lost to the immensity. There were villages back there in that dark, lush expanse that had never seen a white man until the 1950s, and they still lived in the same primitive fashion as their ancestors.

Nonetheless…the good news was, Will, who shared the cockpit with me, suddenly spotted the smidgen of a tail jutting out of the leafy expanse. There was so little showing it was no surprise that search flyers had missed it. Actually, it was the low angle at which we approached, and the illumination from the touch of a rising sun that forced the jungle to surrender its latest victim.

"That's it!" my partner yelled. "That's it!"

I got a couple of the tail numbers and Travis saved some coordinates in his GPS.

"It's Eddie's!" I cried.

There was a burble of excitement and a handful of exclamations not fit for Sunday brunch as I brought the aircraft around and sat it down in the brown-green river about a quarter-mile from the wreckage.

An hour later, we had forced our way through a surly, uncooperative jungle. We were sweat-soaked, exhausted, and had fought off generations of mosquitoes, but there before us emerged Eddie's Grumman Goose. Or what was left of it. The plane had burned, or at least, much of it had. Some of the fuselage survived. The tail caught the least damage but the middle of the plane, closest to the wing tanks and the cockpit, was charred to the point of being almost unrecognizable. We forced ourselves to check but we couldn't find a body. That didn't actually mean much because as soon as everything cooled, the jungle scavengers would have dragged away anything...edible.

There was no satisfaction in what we found and no real closure. In the end, we were left with the only logical conclusion. Our friend was gone.

CHAPTER NINE

It was mid-morning on a beautiful day — a warm sun, a few soft clouds, a blue sky, and a calm green river taking him where he wanted to go. Silvano Petros was enjoying himself. He was only about a day or two out of Caracas now. From the Tuy River, he had entered the Rio Guaire and it was treating him like a kind mother. She would carry him just to the east side of Caracas, where he would anchor up for a day or two and sell a portion of the diamonds. Then, from there, it was only about a day's run into Maiquetia and the convent. His new companions, the dog and the sea hawk, seemed to have settled in with him. Even his cat had cautiously accepted them. The hawk came and went with stoic independence. He needed nothing but he often threw a fish or a hare on the deck and cocked his head for a moment, those sharp, hard eyes staring at the old riverman. Then the bird would lift off again in a swift, indifferent movement, offering a quick call. He slept on the heavy radio antenna mounted on the top of the forecastle.

The dog was up and around now, moving without much indication of pain. The truth was, he had been pummeled badly, but his lacerations weren't nearly as bad as they had appeared in the beginning. The wound on his side had closed and the battering he had received left no indications of serious injury. For all intents and purposes, he was back in "the game of life."

Petros had given the whole thing some serious thought — about giving not just a couple, but the great majority of the diamonds to the nuns in the mission. It was a hard thing for an old thief to do but it was a good thing. It might even negate enough of the bad he'd done to get him into Heaven.

Si...esta possible...

And he could certainly use all the help he could get when he got to the other side. He chuckled to himself. Even with death, he was trying to hedge his bets.

Unfortunately, it was about that time that Silvano's previous immorality got in the way of his present good luck. As he worked his way down the placid green-brown river and smoked a cigar, hands lightly on the wheel of his old jungle trader, thinking about how rich and happy he was going to be, Petros heard a plane approaching.

"That's him!" growled Santiago, the diamond cutter, sitting next to the pilot in the old, beefed-up Cessna 172 floatplane.

The two guys in the back instinctively shifted their hands to their rifles.

"That's him. I know the old bastard's boat!"

"So, how do we do this?" asked one of the men from the back seat.

Santiago nudged the pilot. "Take it down. Put us on the water behind the boat and just stay close behind it. We'll get out on the pontoons and put a few dozen rounds through the stern and the engine housing. We want to stop the bastard first." He held up a forefinger. "No killing him until we get the diamonds."

Petros put the boat on automatic pilot (they were in a wide, straight section of the river) and moved to the stern, his new dog companion following him. He watched the plane touch down on the placid river and begin to push its way closer. It was about a hundred yards out, but steadily moving in. Suddenly, two men exited the plane and moved out onto the pontoons. They carried rifles. Oddly enough, Petros could hear a second plane now, coming in from the south, above and behind the others.

"This is not good..." he whispered to himself. "This is not good..."

He had no sooner turned toward the wheelhouse when there was a staccato burst of gunfire from the men on the Cessna's pontoons, and he could hear the wood at the stern shatter and split. He was stumbling forward, along the starboard rail, toward the throttle and the wheel, when a second burst ripped through the exterior cabin wall next to him.

Part of the problem here was Silvano Petros's instinctive dislike of guns. All he owned was an old revolver that he kept in the wheelhouse, but it hadn't been cleaned or oiled in a year. *Better than nothing...* He stumbled along the port walkway, entered the cabin, ripped open the drawer, and grabbed the gun as another burst of automatic fire ripped through the old lapstrake hull near the stern. The engine sputtered and died, pretty much along with Petros's chances of survival.

As everything went quiet and the old trawler turned sideways, drifting listlessly, Petros and his new dog cautiously exited the cabin and eased their way back toward the stern.

"This is not good," he whispered to the dog. "This is not good. Who would want to hurt this old trader?" he muttered. Then he shrugged, offering a bitter smile. "That is probably a stupid question..." He reached up and intuitively touched the locket at his neck.

He was right. Santiago Chias was already growling at the pilot to pull up close enough to the drifting boat to board it.

The trip back to Caracas had been nearly silent and sadly retrospective, given the eyes of my companions — staring out blindly at the passing landscape, numbed by the realization of our loss and the constant vibration of the plane.

We were cruising along at a thousand feet, pretty much following the river back, lost to our individual introspections and recollections of a wildly crazy, courageous, damned incredible man. Unfortunately, there was nothing anyone could say that could change a thing.

But at that moment, my copilot, Will, pointed downriver at an old trawler of some sort. He pulled me out of my stupor and I realized that something was very wrong with the scene below — a single-engine Cessna was chasing the boat on the water, and it appeared there were men on the pontoons firing at the battered old craft.

"Whoa, dude. That ain't right..." I hissed as I instinctively dropped our Cessna down toward the melee and made a flyby at about a hundred feet off the water.

One pass was enough to get the picture. Three men in a Cessna floatplane on the water were shooting the crap out of the old trawler. It appeared the trader's engine had been taken out. There was lots of smoke back there.

We were familiar with the idea of river pirates in South America. We'd been there and done that. I cranked the plane around hard and turned around a second time, coming in just off the water to the port side of the boat. This time I saw a man — an older guy, waving a pistol by one of the rails. There was a dog by his side — a big dog — a German shepherd mix...

Just like...

I shook my head and looked again but we were already past the boat and I was throwing us into a tight wingover turn to get back to the scene.

The boat below was getting seriously shot up. The plane on the water had moved in and one of the men on a pontoon was trying to toss an anchor over the stern rail. It was about then that I caught a glimpse of the most amazing damned thing. The old guy and his dog had retreated to the interior for a moment, and as one of the bad guys was trying to board over the stern, a gray-and-white lightning bolt with talons suddenly fell out of the sky and in a brutal three seconds, redesigned the man's hairline. He screamed and fell overboard into the river, and the hawk lifted away into the air again.

I kept the impossible scene in view for as long as I could. *For God's sake! Cielo! It had to be Cielo!*

I heard Jing, who was on my side of the aircraft, cry out — *scream* was more accurate — the name of her hawk. She too had witnessed it.

"Good God," I whispered, trying to get another look at the dog. *"Good God!* Shadow..." It was impossible. I *knew* it was impossible — the coincidence was off the charts. But every man has a right to hope when reality says you're crapped out. Hope is the only thing stronger than fear...

I swung the aircraft around in a neck-snapping roll — way beyond the structural limits for the floatplane design and eliciting cries from the generally stoic Travis and Cody in the back — bringing it back around for another pass, then dropping in and slapping the floats down on the slow, green river.

We were just in time to witness another of the men in the plane boarding the boat. He was a tallish, older man, but he moved with purpose. The guy had barely gotten over the rail when, from out of the stern, came the dog. He hit the intruder full on, in midair. All the damned creature needed was a cape… The fellow screamed like a child and lost his rifle, throwing up his hands and stumbling backward as he and the dog went over the rail and into the river. There is no fighting a monster German shepherd and swimming at the same time. In less than ten seconds, the guy broke away from the dog and set out for shore like a madman. As the animal paddled back toward the trawler, the pilot of the plane had seen enough. He cut the mooring line and stumbled back into his cockpit. He did have the integrity to pick up his two passengers, who were drifting downriver, then they were gone, into the air.

As I taxied toward the old trawler, I saw the dog fighting the current back to the big boat. I quickly swung over and brought the plane ahead of him, letting it float over to the animal. *I knew it was Shadow. I knew it was!* I crawled out onto a pontoon and knelt, arms out, calling to him. His head jerked up and he swung around. One look and he was barking furiously, heading my way. In seconds, my boy was out of the water and in my arms, moaning and whining and licking my face as we balanced on the pontoon. I thought I'd died and gone to Heaven. I had held hope and I had lost it, and I had prayed…Lord, had I prayed. But in the end, it just seemed so impossible…

I also had the distinct pleasure of witnessing the remarkable reunion of Jing and Cielo. A few moments after the commotion was over, and the bad guys' aircraft was headed away, Jing stood on a pontoon and whistled, loud and clear, crying out strange words that none of us understood. She had donned her leather gauntlet on a forearm to protect fragile flesh against the crushing power of Cielo's talons. There was an immediate reply from above us, where the bird was circling. The sea hawk dropped in a nosebleed dive, flaring out at the last moment and gracefully, with the flutter of those immense, powerful wings, landed on his mistress's arm. You could feel an energy there — ancient, powerful, and abiding — as she spoke to her companion in a long-lost language and pulled him close. And the immense, remarkably dangerous creature cooed like a child at the breast and rubbed against her.

There are some things, some scenes in life, you just remember, etched in poignant, extraordinary emotion outside the bounds of the commonplace. That was one for me…

This whole thing was just beyond coincidence. I didn't understand it but at this point, I didn't care. I didn't care who or what orchestrated it. I would take it. I would gladly, thankfully, take the magnificent gift the gods had granted me.

I couldn't help remembering an old pilot friend of mine then — a "midnight runner" who got out of the business while the getting was still good. He had seen his share of flukes and chance and luck. One night at a bar we were talking about surviving...and chance. He turned to me and said, "Have you ever considered how boring the world would be without coincidence? And how important that particular element is?" He smiled. "I've heard it said that coincidence is God's way of remaining anonymous. Could be." He eased out a sigh. "I've known people who simply didn't believe in a higher power. I will tell you this: I have nothing against anyone who doesn't believe in God. It's not my business. But from what I've seen, atheists are not generally lucky people. Maybe that's why they're atheists." He shrugged. "And maybe that's why they're unlucky..."

I never forgot that.

I also remembered what Rufus once said. *"Luck, coincidence, timing — dey seem to be mon's explanations for de wiles of de gods... But I say dis to you. Da more you pay attention to dese kindnesses — da more you touch a finger to your chest, den point at da sky with a thankful smile afterward...da more dey happen. Ya mon... It be called 'priming da pump of luck.' True dat, mon..."*

We spent the afternoon helping the old guy who owned the trawler. By some miracle, the engine block on the boat survived the attack. A couple of hoses had been blown apart, which had caused the shutdown, and he'd taken a few rounds here and there, but all above the waterline. The fellow, Silvano Petros, was incredibly thankful for our arrival and assistance, but he was clearly disappointed to be surrendering Shadow. He said he would miss the dog greatly but the hawk scared him, and he would miss it less. He told us about the epic battle with the big cat in the jungle, and the days afterward, while Shadow healed, and I was grateful for his kindness.

When we asked him about the guys in the floatplane, he got sort of a weird look, then shrugged. "Probably bandits," he said cautiously, his eyes doing a little dance that I didn't like. "But I thank you so much for saving this innocent old trader, who has so little to interest bandits to begin with…"

And so it was that we flew away no more the wiser, and Silvano Petros rode off into the sunset to sell the stones he'd stolen from a man who had stolen them from someone else. *A thief who steals from a thief is pardoned for a hundred years.* Or so they say, south of the border…

Speaking of south of the border…

Before banking his newfound wealth and buying tickets for him and his cat to Mexico, Petros somewhat reluctantly kept his word to the god he knew the best, and the nuns of the Mother of Hope Mission in Maiquetia, Venezuela, became rich beyond their meager dreams. In the months to come, there was a new wing built onto the monastery, as well as a small but real infirmary. The food improved immensely, and they were able to hire a part-time doctor for the children. All because of a thief with a newfound conscience…

Ain't the world an amazing place?

CHAPTER TEN

We returned to Caracas full of disappointment regarding our incredible friend, Crazy Eddie. I couldn't believe it. I couldn't accept it. Throughout the time that I had known Eddie, he'd become bigger than life to me — taking chances that would curl the hair of the bravest men, always seeing the angle, and always playing it to perfection. *Pilot extraordinaire...* I couldn't believe he was gone.

But on the other side of the coin, we had miraculously found Shadow and Cielo. That was truly nothing short of an act of God, and in that respect, my faith was restored. But in truth, we hadn't accomplished our goal for being here at all — the crystal skulls and the possibility of a crevice on the side of a cliff denoted by *a mote in a God's eye.* Or so they said...

We paid for the plane rental and the vehicle Travis and Cody had rented, then took a taxi back to our motel and packed. No one felt like going out for dinner. The following morning, we took a taxi to the airport and made the long flight back to the Keys in Cody's Cessna 310.

It was a crowded, slightly over-grossed trip (with a fueling/bathroom stop in Jamaica) and everyone welcomed the sandy earth beneath our feet when we reached Key West. After securing the aircraft and doing a quick Customs process, everyone got their gear, and without too much ado, we went our separate ways. We were all just too exhausted and too damned disheartened for much more.

Somehow, the news people at the *Key West Citizen* had gotten word of the loss of Eddie, and the paper the next day carried a brief front-page article, mostly of assumptions. We all had refused interviews. We did, however, start to plan a wake at Crazy Eddie's Bar and Swill. Our friend would have liked that.

There was one person who read the article on Eddie and his friends with more than just a passing interest.

Bill Simpson, the Smithsonian "contact" for South Florida, drove down to the Keys from Miami, bought a paper, and casually talked to a few people. He highlighted parts of the news piece and placed a call.

"Yes sir, that's right. It appears one of them was killed when the plane went down in the jungle. The others survived. But it doesn't look like they accomplished anything of interest there. They never even made it over to the area of significance. Yes sir, I'll keep you posted."

After a good night's sleep in my own bed, I felt a little better, but I awoke to the same sad truths. Eddie was gone and all our lives were changed for the worst because of it. Shadow was already out and about, back in his environment and, I was certain, out doing a "wander" — checking everything to his satisfaction, re-peeing on his boundaries. After some coffee, I called Travis to discuss the "celebration of life" for Eddie at his bar. The whole town expected it, I was sure.

At midday, the team met at the bar to do a little planning for the party our buddy would surely expect, wherever he was. I left Shadow at home, free to roam. He would probably hook up with Cielo at some point during the day. They were that connected. The hawk could fly the handful of miles between them in a blink.

The wake planning went smoothly, mainly because it wasn't about anything fancy. A few words were to be offered by Eddie's closest friends, a story or two to be told, and free drinks for a couple of hours in memory of an extraordinary fellow. We planned it for Friday night, three days away. Afterward, I caught up on a few errands in Key West — paid some bills, got some cash from the bank. By the time I got home, the sun was nearing the horizon and Shadow was coming out of the mangroves along the water. Life was almost good. *Almost...*

Eddie's celebration of life was a huge success, if you can say that about wakes. Wonderful stories were told about an exceptional man — tales that would have been considered outright lies and imagination if you didn't know the fellow. Will had found a wonderful shot of Eddie standing by his Goose, and we had it enlarged and hung over the bar.

But the best part came at the end of the night, when everyone was pretty well lit. Travis and Cody did something amazing. Someone had purchased a brass urn for Eddie, which was supposedly meant to sit at the back of the bar, in front of the big mirror. Travis got up and pulled a loop or two of white nylon anchor line from his pocket. He and Cody went over to the urn and as they did, things began to quiet down. Travis just did that — people just automatically paid attention to the man. He grabbed the urn, popped off the lid, and tossed it on the bar. Then he tied the small piece of nylon rope around the bottom lip of the urn, leaving a small loop at the other end. Then he stretched up and hung it, upside down, on an eyehook in the ceiling, in front of the mirror and over the liquor bottles. He turned to everyone. The place had gone totally quiet now. Everybody was watching.

It was Cody's turn then. He stepped forward and brought out his hands like an old-time preacher. "This urn will remain upside down and empty until someone shows me proof positive that my friend is gone!" he shouted. "Until that time, he is MIA and he lives on — in our hearts and in this bar! Not to be forgotten!"

There was a pause, then Cody shouted "Oorah!" — the U.S. Marine Corps battle cry. He brought his arms up high. "Oorah! Eddie!"

Immediately, there was a response from Travis and the vets in the bar. "Oorah! Oorah, Eddie!"

Then the rest of the crowd picked it up and the rafters shook with the honoring and the memory of an absolutely extraordinary man.

Rinco Rodriguez watched the ceremony from the back of the room. He raised his glass and whispered "Oorah, Eddie... *Semper Fi.* Oorah..."

In the end, most everyone got seriously drunk and it took a day just to put the bar back in order.

For the next week or so things were relatively quiet. Everyone was recovering from our latest experience, and of course, the loss of Eddie. Shadow and I were taking a lot of long walks along the mangrove passageways that led to the bay. Will called a few times to make sure I was okay. I was having a hard time getting out of this funk — a really hard time. It was as if we had left things half done and lost a comrade at the same time, and we never even got near to our goal of finding the lost crystal skull.

Even Cody mentioned the same thing to me when I ran into him in Key West the following day. "I need something to get my mind off of this," he said. "I need a win…"

"Yeah, me too," I replied. "I need to get back on the horse. I need something to throw myself into."

There was a pause and he looked at me, his blue eyes narrowing in agreement. "You know, you're right. We need to get back on the horse." He exhaled hard. "Maybe we need to go back to Venezuela and find that damned crystal skull. A good adventure would take our minds off of…*things*…"

It wasn't like I hadn't thought about it. I shrugged. "Yeah… Yeah, mon! You know, that might be just the ticket. Besides, I've been having sort of an intuition that's been pulling me back to that. A job undone and the possibility of…something extraordinary…"

"I'm going to talk with Travis," Cody said. "You get in touch with Will and the kids. Let me know what they think. We didn't get an adventure this last time — it was a debacle, and it left me with a bad taste in my mouth." He drew a breath. "I don't like losing at anything."

But something happened that slightly delayed another adventure — actually, it was somewhat of an adventure in itself, and in the process, I was introduced to another Key West character.

Rinco Rodriquez had read the *Citizen* article with the deepest of sadness. That old pirate, Crazy Eddie, had been one of his heroes — and a guy like Rinco didn't have many heroes. He eased out a heavy breath. There was nothing he could do there and he had his hands full with a ring of lousy bastards who killed dogs for sport. He had to stop them before the next "contest." But before he could do much one way or another, a new development changed the situation dramatically.

That evening, when I pulled onto the concrete pad under my stilt house, there was no sign of Shadow. It wasn't all that unusual, especially given the fact that we'd been gone for a while. I made myself some supper — a TV dinner and a beer — then relaxed out on the porch, slapping mosquitoes, drinking a second beer, and watching the disappearing sun turn the sky to gold. I couldn't help but sigh.

But by the time I was done and the sun had slipped away, and the veil of evening was creeping over the landscape, there was still no Shadow. I began to walk out a ways, calling, not too concerned yet. We'd been gone a while. Maybe my boy was just catching up a bit.

By ten o'clock, I was getting worried. This was totally out of character. I called Jing. She said Cielo had shown up about seven-thirty.

"I thought it was strange. Cielo was out of sorts a little... fidgety..." she told me. "He didn't settle into his cage like normal — he disappeared for a while, then came back, but he didn't seem right."

My stomach did a little flip flop and I could suddenly feel the pulse at my temples. "Thanks," I said. "Keep me posted if you hear anything."

My boy didn't come home that night, and by morning I was bleary-eyed from almost no sleep and worried to hives. I spent the day driving up and down our area of the Keys, along the highway and the backroads, and all the mangrove back tracks, but there was no sign of him. By afternoon, I was freaking out. I called the local Animal Control people, and *The Key West Citizen* and *The Keynoter* about ads, but it would be the day after tomorrow with the daily *Citizen*, and four days with the weekly *Keynoter*. I was absolutely panicking. I didn't know what else to do. Then I remembered about the guy...the guy they called Animal Man. If he paid attention as much as the stories about him said, he might have some insight. An hour later, I was in Sloppy Joe's writing a desperate message at the bottom of the pool table blackboard — that's what people said to do. I left my name. Normally, people didn't do that but I was desperate. The truth was, as a member of the Hole in the Coral Wall Gang, I wasn't exactly unknown in the area.

For the rest of the day, I wandered up and down the Keys, checking every conceivable place that my dog might be. Jing even did that weird, "make your hair stand up" thing she did with Cielo in that strange language and set the hawk loose. I had high hopes there but at the end of the day, I had nothing. Zip. Shadow was gone. By evening time I was mentally exhausted and shaky nervous, standing on my porch again watching another sun die. I couldn't stand the idea. I just couldn't tolerate the thought of...

About that time, the phone rang. I ran inside and snatched it off the cradle. "Yes?"

"Is this Kansas Stamps?" asked the voice.

"Yes, yes it is."

"This is Animal Man," the voice said without any presumptuousness. "I haven't found your dog but I have an idea about what may have happened to him. We need to meet as soon as possible."

"You say where, I'm there."

"How about Mallory Square in an hour — give you time to get down the Keys. Look for a green T-shirt and a Special Forces ball cap."

I was in the car before the clanging of the phone in the cradle faded.

The sun was gone and that dark-gray twilight had taken over. Night was minutes away when I parked. Most of the tourists had slipped away now, fading from the square with the daylight. It didn't take me long to find a guy wearing a green shirt, blue jeans, and a ball cap at the far corner, away from most of the light. *Hmmm.* The fellow was a fairly good-sized man, five eight probably, with a lean, hard-looking build. He moved with confidence. Not a pencil pusher. His hair (that I could see) was dark, military short, and his eyes, though dark, held an odd touch of humanity. He nodded as I approached. We stood facing each other for a moment, then he offered his hand and I shook it.

"I'm sorry for what's taken place with you," he said. "Trust me,

I understand." He eased out a sigh. "I don't generally meet with people so that no one knows who I am, you understand?"

I nodded, not sure where this was going.

He continued. "But you come with a certain...reputation...and I'm hoping I can trust you."

"Don't worry," I said. "All I want is my dog back. You pull that off and we'll be friends forever that never met."

He chuckled and there was a soft glint in his eyes that belayed the initial gruffness. He came right to the point. "I don't know for sure where your dog is, but I think I might know what happened to him. If you've been paying attention to the classifieds in the paper, you might have noticed an unusual number of large dogs have gone missing over the last two or three months."

I shrugged. I hadn't noticed.

The fellow continued. "Here's the tactical intelligence on this situation, just under the radar enough to keep it out of the newspapers. There is a dog-fighting ring operating in the Lower Keys. The operational nexus is out of Haiti, and they still bring dogs in from out of the country, but that's a hassle, so, in the last few months they've begun stealing animals locally — mostly in the upper Keys and the Homestead area." He paused and drew a breath. "But sometimes, when the situation is right and they come across a lone animal that's big enough for combat, they steal locally."

"You mean..."

"Yeah, I think your dog may have been snatched." He sighed heavily and his eyes became worried and hard at the same time. "If they've taken your dog, you have a very short window in which to find him. The fights are to the death, and even a powerful animal usually only lasts two or three fights because they don't give them enough time to heal." Again he hissed out a breath. "Sometimes they deliberately wound them with an ice pick, just before the combat, to throw the fight and rake in even more money."

"Jesus Christ!" I hissed. "How in God's name would they snatch these dogs?" I asked incredulously. "These are big, often mean creatures, and mine is way too smart to buy into a 'steak on a stick' trick."

My new acquaintance shrugged. "They shoot them with anesthetizing darts and quickly drag them into vans. That's what

I'm told." He paused for a moment, as if coming to a decision, then continued. "I've been chasing a ring here. The operators are clever. They rarely hold more than two contests in the same place. They use extra-large storage areas that they rent. They bring in portable bleachers and a portable fence to separate the spectators from the animals. They're in and out in a night or two. They clean up after themselves, so there's no evidence, maybe just some bloodstains on the floor."

"How come you know so much about this?" I asked. "And why haven't you gone to the police?"

"A couple of the local police are in on it — a handful of dollars at the end of the month. And...I might not be able to do what I do if the police knew who I was." The man paused and his eyes went distant for a moment, then he caught himself. "And let's just say I like dogs, okay?"

I nodded. "I'm good with that. So, what do we do?"

"I've found one of their new 'animal holding areas,'" my new friend said. "We can start there. Tomorrow night, if you're up to it." He paused. "You have a non-lethal weapon you prefer?"

I nodded. "I've got a stun gun and a police baton that I'd definitely like to use when we find these folks." I paused. "But if my dog's not...okay...when we find him, you'd better leave..."

I saw a light of appreciation come on in my new friend's eyes. "Fine, brother," he said. "You do what you need to do. I'm good. I'll have your back." He exhaled. "Most of the people who mistreat animals don't have a good, first-hand understanding of the pain they're causing." He offered a thin smile. "I recommend a baseball bat or a handheld taser for...'educational tools.'"

"What do I call you?" I said, starting to like this guy. "I'm gonna need a name if we're going to become partners in melee."

My new acquaintance hesitated for a moment, then sighed, as if making a decision. "Rinco," he said. "My name's Rinco." Then he held out his hand, and as I shook it, he said, "A man should know his brother's name when they go into the fray."

I liked that. It said something about this man...that he'd been there and done that before.

The following night, we again met at Mallory Square. Then the two of us, attired in dark clothes, took Rinco's van and wound around the primary road on Big Coppitt Key until we neared the end. We made a right at the last road, then headed around the edge of the shore to an old conch house with a garage in the back. There was a battered Chevy van out front, with stickers relating to Haiti on the bumper. Island music reverberated from within the house. I drove past for about a quarter-mile and parked. There was just enough moonlight to guide us.

As we circled back to the house, the smell of ganja pervaded the air outside. The door to the garage was locked but that didn't slow us. Rinco elbowed out a windowpane and unlocked it. We stepped inside and the smell took my breath away. There were six dogs, each one in a four-by-four cage, pretty much living in their own waste. They didn't seem emaciated — they'd been fed and they even had their original identification collars. But most importantly, there, in the back cage, was Shadow! He was already whining and barking at me. In the next few moments, I had him out of his wired prison and he was all over me, crying and licking me as I knelt to hold him.

We were just figuring out our next move, and a couple of the other dogs were barking now, when a voice behind us growled, "Who you be, mons? What you be doin' here?"

There in the doorway stood a big, dreadlocked black man waving a large revolver in one hand and holding a bottle of rum in the other. As he stepped into the room cautiously, another man, not quite as large (a frizzy black halo of hair, thin, but hard-looking) stepped in behind him. No visible weapon there...

I grabbed Shadow's collar, keeping him contained. I didn't want him shot.

But suddenly, my new friend threw up his arms, and sliding into a Caribbean brogue, cried, "What I be doin' here, mon? What I be doin' here? What *you* be doin' here is da question. Da bossman gonna be seriously pissed. Jo Jo sends me over to look at your animals an' all I see is dese skinny shit dogs!" Rinco thrust out his hands. "When you feed dem last, mon? When you clean dere cages?" All the time that Rinco was in this act, he was edging closer, his hands in the air, waving about. "You gwena be in deep shit, mon!" he cried. "Da bossman see dis, he likely be blind-bitch mad, mon, and you gwena be in dem got-dam cages!"

The larger man with the gun was startled but not completely sold. He was bringing his gun around hesitantly when my new friend's demeanor suddenly switched. Rinco dropped the Caribbean hand-waving thing, stepped in, and slapped the barrel away with one hand, then reached over and popped the guy with two fingers on the side of his neck, faster than a snake. I mean, the whole thing was totally effortless. Rinco's hand was already back at his side and he was still telling the guy about the trouble he'd bought when the big fellow's eyes went wide, the bottle slipped from his hand, his knees buckled, and he dropped to the ground like a sack of potatoes. His fairly drunk companion had just enough time to realize there was a serious problem when my friend smiled at him, stepped in, and effortlessly "popped" him with those same two fingers on the temple — *truly as fast as a snake...* The guy got a startled look, and he held that look even as he exhaled and crumpled onto the dusty concrete floor.

"What the hell?" I muttered. "What did you just do? Who the hell are you?"

"Explanations later," my friend said. "Right now, we need to get these dogs out of here."

And we did, by backing Rinco's van up against the door to the shed, then opening the cages and shooing the dogs out and into the back of the vehicle. One of the Haitians came to while we were in the process. He was trying to gain his feet when my new friend stepped over and sharply touched him with those two fingers again on the side of the neck. The fellow's eyes widened, he exhaled, then his eyes closed. Bing, bam, boom — that was it. I'd never seen anything like it. It wasn't fighting, it was more like magic. Very spooky...

"We'll take these guys to the Key West Animal Shelter," Rinco said as we drove away. "They'll find the owners." He paused. "It's a win tonight. It's a win. They won't have these dogs to use at the next fight. And you have your boy back."

As we drove, Shadow at my feet in the cab, my curiosity got the better of me. I turned to Rinco, who was at the wheel. "What in the hell did you do to those guys? I've never seen anything quite like that. It was like you touched them and *bang!* they were on the ground..."

Rinco shrugged. "It is an ancient Chinese art of combat." He exhaled softly. "It was called *Jaioli* originally, and goes back as far as 221 BC. Primarily, it involves strikes, mostly pressure point attacks." He paused. "Very effective stuff compared to the karate classes of today. It is almost like using magic."

"No joke," I said. "How did you, an all-American boy, end up learning to use something so...sophisticated?"

My friend sighed and his eyes went distant for a moment. "Long story, actually... But the short version is, ten, twelve years ago, I found myself in Chinatown on one of those cross-country trips young people did more of back then." He paused to collect his thoughts. "I came across a situation in a backstreet — don't actually remember how or why I ended up there, but anyway, I came across three guys who had a young Chinese girl cornered in an alley, and it didn't look like it was going to end well. My American chivalry kicked in and I decided to come to the rescue. I was a fairly capable guy then — had two years of YMCA boxing and I was bigger than my opponents.

"I broke it up for a moment, then I got hit with a two-by-four and all my 'hero' bled out onto the street. I was too dizzy to even stand, but I remember watching what took place next." He paused in recollection and smiled. "Suddenly, this middle-aged Asian guy was standing there. He'd come down the fire escape from an apartment above." Rinco grinned. "The first thing it reminds me of now is that movie, *The Karate Kid*. It was strange, really. He told them to let her go, and they, of course, didn't. One of them held the girl while two of them went over to him. One of those guys suddenly had a knife. When they were close enough and telling the older guy what they were going to do to him, the son of a bitch just smiled. He pointed behind them and said 'police.'"

My buddy got a reminiscent smile. "That word always gets your attention, especially if you're a bad guy. The two alley rats turned to look, just for a second. That was all the old guy needed. I swear, he just stepped in, remarkably fast for a geezer, and just 'touched' the closest one on the neck. Man, it just looked like a touch but the bad guy's eyes blinked, his knees buckled, and he dropped like a rock. The second guy threw a punch. The Chinese fellow didn't even try to block it. He just swayed and the punch missed completely. That was impressive, but what was amazing, what really caught my attention, was his response. Again his arm shot out and with just two fingers, he 'touched' the fellow just above the elbow. The guy's arm just dropped, as if it had been hammered by a two-by-four. The man grunted in shock and pain, and looked up just in time to see the Chinese guy poke him in the jugular. That was it. The fellow's eyes went wide, then they went blank, and he collapsed like a ragdoll."

He grinned at the memory. "That was my introduction to Master Chan Che and the ancient art of *Jaioli*. Long story short, Master Che was impressed with my chivalry and I was impressed with his subtle way of kicking ass. Somehow, we became acquaintances and he decided to teach me a few things. I stayed in San Francisco for three months and became a student of *Jaioli*. Exactly like *The Karate Kid*. The son of a bitch had me cleaning his house and washing his car." Then he offered a cagy smile. "And I would gladly have done it twice for the knowledge. While it was a martial art of sorts, it didn't require years to perfect. It was basically about special exercises for strengthening the first two fingers on each hand — pounding sand, then gravel, then light wood until you had rocks for fingers, then studying human neurology — learning where to hit someone most effectively and practicing your delivery with a few *katas*." Rinco shook his head. "Time well spent. Makes most martial arts look like way too much work."

We dropped the dogs off at the Key West Animal Shelter, and my new friend took Shadow and me back to my truck at Mallory Square. "Tonight was a win," he said as we stood underneath the yellow night lamps and shook hands, preparing to go our separate ways.

I nodded. "Damned right it was." I paused. "And I'm grateful, man. Totally grateful for your help in getting my boy back."

"We were lucky," Rinco replied. "There are a lot of people who aren't so lucky, and there are a lot of dogs..." He paused. "...who aren't lucky at all. We won a battle. We didn't win the war..."

I turned to go, then turned back. "I've got about a week or so before I'm leaving on another trip with my friends. Maybe we could get together, have a drink, talk a little more about this war and this dog-fighting ring."

Rinco smiled. "I'd like that, man. Yeah, I'd like that..."

As I turned again to leave, he added, "Listen, I don't know how far you want to go with this, but the boss of this ring — a big Jamaican they call Chakan — has a well-protected home on the back of Sugarloaf Key. It's where he keeps the top animals in his fighting ring. The ones that make him money." He looked at me and smiled but his eyes were hard as rocks. "I'd like to break this ring once and for all." He paused. "Take 'em out."

"You mean..."

My friend nodded, eyes still hard. "Yeah, probably that's what I mean. We take this Chakan guy out, completely. The hard truth is, we could disable him and his operation so badly, he thinks there's no percentage in operating here." Rinco offered a bitter sigh. "But all that means is he just goes somewhere else."

I have to tell you, I was damned impressed with my new friend. Seriously impressed. However, I knew clearly what he was saying and I wasn't sure I could approach this from that angle here in the States. But I was reminded of what my buddy Travis said on occasion. "Sometimes you gotta do the hard thing so good people can sleep at night. There are really only three kinds of folks — there are sheep, there are wolves, and there are sheepdogs, who keep the wolves from the sheep. At some point in life, you have to decide what you are."

I exhaled heavily. "Let me sleep on it, okay?"

They say timing is everything. I might have just let this go but for an incident the next day. Three wounded dogs — apparently from fights — were found dumped in the mangroves on a back road on Long Key. All of them had been shot to death. Someone's companions, loved and cared for, had been stolen, mutilated for money, and killed because it was too much trouble to fix them. I decided to go see Travis.

CHAPTER ELEVEN

"We don't necessarily have to kill them all," growled Travis, standing on his porch, staring out at the mangrove flats behind his home. "It's like rats — you annoy them badly enough, they leave." He paused and those fiery green eyes gazed off, contemplating. "But you generally have to mess up a few to get the point across. Fire works really well against rats."

Travis just happened to fall into the "animal lover" category as well. Moreover, he hated the changes he was seeing in the Keys. He too remembered the sleepy, peaceful place with cool, good-hearted people. He turned back to me. "You know where their home base is, right?"

I nodded. "Yeah. Big stilt house, all by itself, fenced compound, Sugarloaf Key, on the Gulf side."

"How many combatants can we expect?"

"My friend says maybe six or seven. But they're not expecting any resistance and security is pretty lax."

Travis looked at me. "I'll call Cody. We'll plan for tomorrow night. No use delaying this. I want a recon tonight." He paused and his green eyes narrowed. "I have some thoughts on this." And he did...great thoughts. "I need you to find a pizza delivery sign for a car, and a uniform of some sort," he said. "I'll take care of the rest."

"There's one other thing," I said. "I have a friend I need to invite to this party. He's the one who figured this whole thing out, and while I know we don't invite strangers to our gigs, he deserves to be in on this." I paused. "You of all people would appreciate this guy — ex-military and very...capable."

My big friend chewed on that for a moment. "What branch of service?"

"Marines."

Travis nodded reluctantly. "Okay, do it. But he'd better be capable, as you said."

I held up my hands. "Trust me. No problem there."

I drove into Key West to visit with Will. My buddy was left aghast at my story about Shadow and the other dogs. I told him what we were planning — a shock-and-awe type of thing for the following night.

"There's no reason for you to have to do this," I said. "I mean, you don't have a dog in this fight, so to speak."

Will shrugged. "Naahh, I don't, you're right. But if you're a member of this group, you're in for a penny, in for a pound." He exhaled. "When and where?"

Early that evening, when the sun had already set and darkness had crept across the mangroves, Travis and Cody parked their vehicle a quarter-mile out on the marl road, and working their way through the mangroves, did their recon on the Jamaican's stronghold. It was a large house with a barrel tile roof, about a hundred mangrove-covered yards from the water on the Gulf side. It was built on the cleared marl rock of the Keys and mounted on twelve-foot stilts, then the entire compound was enclosed by an eight-foot chain-link fence. There was a camera security system, but it had been poorly installed, leaving indications of where the camera wiring ran back to the house. There was also another building, closer to the water — high, small windows, a heavy chicken-wire-type opening that ran around the top of the twenty by twenty-foot building, just under the roof awnings. Ventilation. Undoubtedly, this was the holding facility for the animals. They both saw a dead dog, someone's friend, just outside the fence at the edge of the mangroves, gathering flies.

Two armed guards were lounging around under the house, and there was one at the gate. Every once in a while, one or the other did a perimeter check of the cleared compound. This whole affair was down to a routine and no one was paying much attention.

Travis looked at his friend. "I don't see a problem."

"It's a go," grated Cody. "Let's fix these sons of bitches."

The following day, Travis rented a large van. I snatched a couple magnetic Pizza Pan Pizza signs off of a delivery vehicle and talked the owner of the local restaurant into selling me an official Pizza Pan Pizza shirt. Later that afternoon, per Travis's instructions, I bought two bottles of heavy-duty sleeping pills and crushed all the pills into a fine powder. Then I purchased two six-packs of beer and two large cheese pizzas. I spread the powdered pills on the hot pizzas, donned my new business shirt, and as the sun began to set, I slapped the magnetic signs on my car and headed for the Jamaican stronghold on Sugarloaf.

I was met at the gate by a big guy with skin like black felt, eyes hard as marbles, a Bob Marley T-shirt, and a pistol tucked into his belt under the shirt. I could see one other guard at the back of the compound, near the path that led to the water.

"Welcome, and good eating from Pizza Pan Pizza!" I said as I pulled up a receipt I had written on the company receipt pad (which I had snatched while buying the pizzas). "Two large cheese with extra sauce and two six-packs of Miller."

The guard looked at me, then back toward the house. "I don' know nothing about no pizza."

"Look," I said congenially. "I don't know any more than you. I just deliver. You don't want them, it's no skin off my nose."

The guy looked back at the house — a good seventy-five yards from the gate — then back to me, then down to the beer on the seat.

"It's only ten bucks man," I added congenially. "Company special this week. Two pizzas, ten bucks. The beer is an extra ten." I paused as the guy stared at me, then back at the house again. It was a long walk to check about a pizza. "The order guy is new, maybe I got the wrong address, but for twenty bucks you've got dinner and drinks..."

The dark islander huffed, then ripped a twenty off a roll of bills. I handed him the pizzas and beer, then rode off into the sunset, literally.

Cody, Travis, and the rest of the team were waiting for me in the parking lot of the Sugarloaf Lodge, just off U.S. Highway 1.

"Mission accomplished," I said.

Travis nodded and looked at Cody. "Let's give them a half hour," he said. "Let the beer and the pills start to work."

And indeed they did.

Thirty minutes later, we parked Rinco's van and our vehicle about a quarter-mile out and moved in on foot, down the sides of the mangrove-lined marl road. Evening was slipping in now, and the shadows were growing. Rinco had explained that we were looking for an extraordinarily heavy Jamaican albino, like a walking refrigerator — pale, milky skin, maybe five foot eight or ten, with green eyes and a yellowish afro. He was our target. The guard was still at the gate, two cans of beer at his feet, but he was leaning sloppily against the chain link, blinking a lot and shaking his head.

Cody was about to move in when Rinco held up a hand. "I'll take this," he said.

Travis hesitated. This guy was an unknown commodity for him and he didn't like mistakes.

I smiled. "Let him have it. Trust me, it's okay."

And it was. Rinco strolled up to the entrance like he owned the place. The man on the outside of the gate straightened up, hand sliding toward his spine where he kept his pistol. But he shook his head slightly, as if he was having trouble focusing.

"Greetings, mon!" said Rinco congenially, stopping about four feet from the guy. "How about we play a game? I bet you ten bucks I can knock you out before you reach that gun," he said, nodding at the man's waist.

The guy's eyes narrowed and he blinked a couple times. He shook his head slightly, then went for the pistol. All Rinco did was step in and flash out a hand, pointing with those two deadly fingers. It was as if he barely touched the arm above the elbow as the guy's hand came up. The Haitian's eyes flinched, his arm fell limp at his side, and the pistol dropped to the marl road. He looked down at his hand, then up at his antagonist, curiosity and shock filling his face. Rinco snapped out again and touched him under the chin. It seemed too fast and light to make much difference but the results were remarkable. The guy's face went blank, his knees buckled, and he dropped face-first into the dirt. Rinco turned and looked back at us and smiled, then motioned a military "come-along."

Travis looked at Cody. His friend, who was also a martial arts expert, grinned. "That's pretty good," he said. "I liked that."

Keeping to the shadows on the sides of the mangroves, we moved into the complex. There was another guard downstairs, under the stilt house. He saw us and was raising a rifle. There was no choice. Cody tapped him twice with a silenced .22 caliber rifle. No noise at all, just a "piffftt." The games were over. It was down to ugly business — time to relocate some rats.

There were at least three other guards in the compound. Two more downstairs and one upstairs. The second one downstairs was just coming out from the building behind the stilt house. As soon as he saw us, he was raising a pistol, no questions asked, no quarter given. It wasn't the way we wanted it but there wasn't much choice. He was dead before he got the gun up.

Travis, silenced rifle at his shoulder, motioned at the stairs of the house with the barrel of his weapon. Rinco didn't hesitate. He brought his M14 up and took the lead. He was locked into grim payback. All the nice had drained away.

The last guy upstairs heard the commotion and came out the door on the deck. The moment he saw us, he scrambled across the deck for the back of the house. But the son of a bitch tripped on a table leg, stumbled into the porch rail, and tumbled over it with a shriek. He hit the concrete pad headfirst. There was an audible crack and his shocked eyes announced he'd just booked a ticket to hell.

Still, Will bent down and checked his pulse, then looked up at us. "Sometimes da gods, dey give you exactly what you deserve," he muttered.

In less than ten minutes, we had cleared the compound of visible assailants and checked on the imprisoned dogs in the smaller building — six animals, in fairly good condition — but there was no sign of the guy we were looking for, the big albino "refrigerator."

We couldn't have known but once again that old expression, "timing is everything," had played a role here. Chakan and two of his men had just berthed their eighteen-foot Aquasport at the small dock at the end of the mangroves, a couple hundred yards from the house, and were coming into the compound along the mangrove trail when they heard the commotion and people shouting. They had been checking some traps for lobster, for which the giant man had a fondness.

By the time they stumbled into the compound, it was obvious that they were too late. Rinco had given my friends and me a description of the unusual Jamaican. Cody, nearest to the mangroves at the back of the house, spotted the man and his companions, and raised his rifle. He knocked down one of Chakan's men, but he was only wounded and continued to return fire. The Jamaican was a quick study. The compound was lost, his men taken out. He was lumbering back toward the boat in a heartbeat, while his wounded soldier, near the mouth of the trail, held the *blancs* at bay. But it turned out Chakan's soldier wasn't all that courageous, and after a few rounds, he too was limping back down the trail. Unfortunately, he wasn't quite fast enough to dodge the rounds from Cody's rifle. He did, however, provide just enough time for Chakan and his other companion to get to the Aquasport, untie the moorings, and run.

We stood at the edge of the mangroves, offering a few angry shots and watching the boat speed away. The huge man had the wheel, and his companion was firing back from the stern. When he thought they were out of range, Chakan drew back on the throttle. The gunman stood defiantly and raised a middle finger at us, shouting what could only have been a combination of curses and challenges, then brought his gun up again. He shouldn't have. He had survived this. But his ego got in the way of intelligence.

Travis exhaled, raised his rifle, aimed, and took a breath, holding it long enough for the report to become a surprise. The guy at the back of the boat jerked, definitely surprised, his arm fell in a listless motion, his rifle dropped, and he tumbled off the stern into the wake.

Cody turned to Travis. "You've been back to the range again, haven't you?"

Travis just shrugged. "I get bored easily."

Chakan hit the throttle on the boat and disappeared.

We took the animals from the shed and put them in the back of the van. They were basically in good shape — these were new, high-potential combatants and they had been given more care than most. But most importantly, they were still somebody's pets.

We picked up all the shell casings from around the area and put the dead bodies in the house as if they were sitting in chairs or lying in bed. Then we used the gas from the generator to burn the wooden house to the concrete pilings. The truth probably wouldn't escape a patient forensics guy, but this was the Keys, not New York.

We were headed south, down U.S. 1, nearly back into Key West, as the fire trucks were speeding northward. Cody made a call to the Key West Animal Shelter and told them we were coming. When we arrived, Rinco made up a story about finding the dogs in an abandoned storage area — no food, no water. That, and a few hundred dollars, was enough to get the animals through the doors.

That was the good news.

The bad news was the one guy we had missed at the house on Sugarloaf, who had been fishing in the flats when the shit hit the fan. When he heard the commotion, he had moved in and watched silently from the mangroves. A single minute of observing the precision of the *blancs* told him there was no percentage in being a hero. He didn't know any of the invaders but he did recognize one man — the tallish Latin *gringo*. Rinco had tasered the fellow when the guy was serving as the doorman at one of the animal fights.

Yes, the fellow knew that man and he already hated him. This destruction was icing on the cake. "Your time soon come, mon," he hissed. "I pray to my god, Bondye, for the power of revenge."

CHAPTER TWELVE

There's nothing like success at a little dangerous entertainment to make you appreciate survival. Yes, unfortunately, lives had been taken, and that's never a comfortable thing. When it becomes easy, you're in trouble. But the individuals the team had dealt with were monsters, born of a dysfunctional society that had lost its "roots" and become a violent social and cultural anomaly in a basically peaceful Caribbean. Now, here in the Keys of all places, some of the dregs of this culture had settled in, then began to brutalize and kill creatures without conscience — for entertainment, of all things — and they had, also without conscience, eliminated the people who got in their way.

The trouble with moving someplace new is that we inevitably bring all that we are with us.

The team hoped that this message would drive this vanguard of criminals out of the Keys. Sometimes the only thing the violent understand is violence.

The good news was, after a few days of watching our backs for potential revenge, things appeared to have settled down. And after catching our collective breath, we began to consider our original plan of slipping down to Venezuela to see if there was really anything to the legendary cave and this crystal skull thing. Will thought the idea of investigating the possibility of the crystal skull was a good venture. He was already on the fringes of boredom and this seemed like a nice, relatively non-lethal adventure.

Tax and Jing didn't have to be asked twice. They were effortlessly evolving into adventure junkies. Cody was between women, and he was in. He contacted Travis, who was missing his overseas girlfriend more than he liked and had nothing to occupy his time. He'd reloaded all the ammunition he could possibly use, did a couple of bone-fishing gigs in the Gulf flats, and tied more new flies than he'd use all year. Our friend rolled those heavy shoulders. "What the hell, man. Sure. What's the worst that can happen?"

I hate it when people use that expression...

Hell, we all knew it was a long shot — a legend told by an old, half-drunk shaman. But it was based on numerous finds across the Southern Hemisphere, some of which could not be explained away by religion or politics. We'd chased our tails for less on occasion, and we all needed to get away from the Keys and let things "cool" a little. Besides, I liked Latin women, and Venezuela was famous for its remarkable rums.

We were sitting around a table at Eddie's, making preliminary plans, when Will said, "You know, maybe we should invite our new friend, Rinco."

Cody shrugged. "I gotta admit, he's...capable. A pretty good man."

Travis smiled, seeing where this was going. "He's an ex-Marine. Can't be all bad."

There were nods from the rest of us.

"I'll call him," I said. "See if he's interested."

"We're thinking about doing one of our gigs down in Venezuela. Looking for an ancient artifact — a lost crystal skull," I said over the phone. "The team got to talking and we thought you might like to join us on a more benign adventure."

"For real, huh?" Rinco said cautiously. "You want me to go with you?"

"If you want. I mean, it may not fit into your plans. We'll be gone for maybe —"

"Where and when?" my friend said, interrupting me. "You tell me when and where and I'll be there with bells on."

"No bells," I replied. "We don't like attention."

There was a soft chuckle at the other end, then with a feigned military demeanor, "Sir, yes sir. No bells."

Two days later, the Hole in the Coral Wall Gang met at Eddie's for "plans." It would take us a few days to put all our ducks in their rows — food, supplies, equipment, radios, plenty of heavy-duty nylon rope for rappelling down cliffs, and a few things that go bang. (Although we had to be very discreet there — small stuff only.) I immediately missed Eddie's Goose with all its incredible hiding places. And then I missed Eddie...

We set a departure date for Friday. We decided to take two planes so the trip over wouldn't be crowded — Cody's 310 Cessna and my Cessna 182 floatplane. This combination also gave us the ability to access more places once we were there. It was a serious damned scavenger hunt at best. But it was clearly better than staying at home and watching "Sanford and Son" reruns.

Like our old friend, Eddie, always said: *"Any excuse is acceptable for sex and adventure..."*

Friday morning, as our two planes lifted off and picked up a southerly heading toward a pale, blue-gold horizon, the Smithsonian's local contact, Bill Simpson, watched from the airport perimeter fence. He picked up his new portable phone and dialed a number. "They're on their way again. Flight plan says Caracas, Venezuela, but I'll bet that's just the first stop." He sighed. "I'm thinking this gig is about the crystal skull."

On the other end of the line, Smithsonian Director Richard Thomason exhaled, not a happy camper. He and his organization were going to have to deal with this bunch of hard-assed adventurers again. The gang's reputation preceded them. People who got in their way inevitably ended up with adjusted mindsets or serious health issues. "Book a flight, pull two men out of Miami and get down there, right away. I want to know everything they do — from what they eat to where they spit."

He hated to admit it but there was something about this crystal skull issue in Venezuela that made him nervous. Most of what had been found already could be explained away or successfully debunked in some fashion. But there were a couple of instances over the last thirty or forty years — one in Central America that came from deep in the interior of a Guatemalan Mayan pyramid, and one found in the ruins of Machu Picchu in the Eastern Cordillera of southern Peru — that carried such an "intensity" and validity about them that the best his people could do was hound the owners with threats of artifact fraud and theft to the point of ceasing any public promotion. Then there was the one in the basement of the Smithsonian. That one just made him purely uncomfortable. It was as if it had a discerning intellect about good and bad. It made him feel like an altar boy who had stolen the Sunday offerings.

The director eased out another breath and hung up the phone. The code name with the agency for this type of incident was

Roswell. "Contradict, disavow, disengage." That was the company's mantra. His agency's job had long since deteriorated from the discovery and preservation of legitimate finds to maintaining a religious and scientific status quo in world society. The planet was just too precariously balanced now. People were too psychologically challenged, too vulnerable and unstable to permit new information that could shatter the existing state of affairs with religion, science, or history. "Hide it, bury it, make it disappear..." That's what his bosses in Washington had told him. And no one cared how he did it, just as long as the hoopla didn't make it to the six o'clock news.

I settled back into the pilot's seat as we rose, the hum of the big Lycoming 0-540 engine offering a slightly noisy comfort, and Key West sliding into a ménage of streets, canals, and bays below us. Will was next to me, flying second seat. An almost bubbling Rinco was in the back with the supplies and equipment. It was a slightly overcast morning but the tropical sun would burn most of that off. In the distance ahead, I could see Cody's sleek 310 winging along, the new sun glistening off its fuselage. The rest of the gang was there — Jing and her hawk, Cielo, and Tax. Cody would have to throttle back a little to keep us together but he understood, no problem...

The whole thing was wrapping up nicely and I was looking forward to another adventurous but not-too-challenging affair. The lady that was Venezuela had taken as much as she'd given on our last trip. I hoped to draw slightly better cards this time. It was still hard not to think about Eddie...not to have him here. Not to know...

We refueled in Haiti. No one left the planes. Not even for a bathroom stop. You just never knew, coming in there. The whole place had a sense of discord about it — a feeling of inconsistency and dissonance. But we all stayed with the plane and it all went without incident. In twenty minutes, we were back in the air. A little over four hours later, both planes were sliding into Simon Bolivar International, which was only a short distance from the Playa Grande Marriott.

We had devised exotic hiding places in both aircraft for the really important things — guns, ammo, etc. So, on we went to the hotel, where we had an excellent dinner, a couple of drinks each, and a relatively good night's sleep. Travis made it clear: "No whore-dogging tonight." We had business to attend to, starting tomorrow. Serious business.

What we didn't know was Bill Simpson and his two Smithsonian heavies had landed in Caracas just three hours behind us.

By ten the following morning, we had spoken with Customs, explaining where we were going. Travis told them that we were coming in to take a battery of photos of the area, perhaps to do a couple of "jumps" for an American magazine. That seemed like a good excuse, and the authorities liked the fact that it was promoting Venezuela. And...Travis had a way about him that discouraged a lot of questions. We were soon piling into the planes, headed for a poorly bulldozed strip at the top of an ocean cliff just west of Boca de Uchire.

The bad news was, the landing proved to be really...*bouncy.* Damned near scary, getting into that "miserable, piece-of-shit runway," as Travis described it, with Cody's twin-engine. The good news was, Cody stopped his aircraft about fifty yards short of going off the cliff that faced the sea. There were several exclamations relating to the landing, none worth repeating. My STOL (Short Takeoff and Landing) Cessna 182 wasn't challenged as much.

Within a couple of hours, we had found a comfortable spot just off the runway, at the edge of the jungle, for a camp, and had thrown up a few small tents — one for Travis and Cody, one for Jing and Tax, and one for Rinco, Will, and me. No one said the words but I know we all felt the specter of Eddie. We missed that gruff voice and the natural insight he offered, and the occasional off-colored anecdote that always broke the tension of a new gig. There was a part of me — a deep intuitive part of me — that wouldn't let him go. I felt like he was there, somewhere... Maybe in the wind or the trees or the sky. But he was there.

The cliffs that the old shaman had described were relatively close to where we had done the parachute jumping contest the last time we were here. It was then (in mid-jump), that I had glimpsed the weathered, almost imperceptible face in the cliff — the one the shaman said with "the cave eye" that contained the last crystal skull of a somewhat benevolent race from beyond the stars. It made a great story if nothing else. I was there at the telling, and I still felt the chance of probability was maybe one in ten. But hey, it was a great excuse for an "easy" adventure, and the truth was, I had felt a connection to this...*concept*...that I couldn't dismiss. I carried the unshakeable conviction about the existence of God. I'd experienced too much extraordinary preservation; I'd heard the voices in the mist in times of peril. I had been "helped" too many times to doubt "spirit." But what I wanted to know, one way or the other, was the truth about this extraordinary theme of other distant races, somewhere out there, and man's remarkable evolutionary ascension on this planet. And just maybe this skull thing was a piece of the puzzle.

I didn't give a tiny rat shit whether I changed someone else's beliefs. That wasn't my job, first off. And secondly, other people's opinions didn't concern me. This was a totally personal thing. Don Quixote had his windmills and I had mine.

After we had set up camp at the edge of the cliffs (a good breeze there, to keep the mosquitoes away), Tax and Jing built a simple latrine behind Cody's twin Cessna and draped a couple of canvas tarps across the starboard wing that faced the camp for privacy. Tax, with his usual exuberance, had dug about a four-foot hole in the sandy loam. It wasn't that wide, but Cody had laughed and told him it was deep enough to trap a cougar, and warned everyone to be careful on their evening "duty."

Jing took her hawk for a jaunt along the cliffs to the west. The big bird soared in and out of the wind currents above and around her — always watching, always protective. Rinco built a first-class fire pit for us and scrounged up some wood for it. Everything seemed to be on target.

The only less-than-pleasing news would have been the two figures hidden in the jungle, with a good view of our camp.

"Son a bitch!" muttered the slightly overweight, smaller one (dark hair, marble-like black eyes), who was attired in a pair of seriously weathered boots, black leather pants and vest, and an equally battered, flat-brimmed Zorro-type hat. "Son a bitch! Dey be back! Payin' dem damn Indians to watch for us paid off."

"You forget that your mother was one of them damn Indians, Carle," gritted his tall, almost gaunt companion, who had a long face, a slightly hooked nose, and large ears that protruded through his shoulder-length, black hair. He looked a great deal like a human fruit bat. All he needed was wings.

The little guy swung around. "How many times I gotta tell you, Ramon, not to call me that. My name is Torro! Torro! My mother may have been an Indian but my father was a dangerous bandito."

"He was a sheepherder."

"No! No! He only did that part-time. When da bandit business was slow."

The tall fellow shrugged. "Okay, Carle, whatever you say... I'm sure the sheep were terrified of him."

"Torro!" barked the diminutive fellow. Torro, Torro, Torro! Chu got ears like a fruit bat and chu still can't hear!"

His nonplussed companion shrugged. "A man hears what he wants to hear..." He sighed. "To business now. We watch and wait. They are back. We know what they have come back for. If they find it, we will steal it."

Torro nodded, calming a bit. "Yeah, stealing is one of the things we do good."

Ramon shrugged. "Possibly the only thing..."

That afternoon we made ten passes along the cliff in question and didn't spot a thing. Flying at just above stall speed against the side of a mountain with dangerous updrafts and downdrafts, in a plane with nearly full tanks, was a challenging affair. (We had topped off the plane when we left Caracas. It was a habit of mine, but not a good choice that day.)

After about a half-hour of sweat-stained, nervous observation, dealing with a mountainside that looked much the same everywhere, we took a break. We had another cup of coffee and talked about it with our friends, with the exception of Jing, who had gone hunting with her hawk. The consensus was, on the first few runs we were too close to get a sense of the image. We decided to give it one more try before we lost the sun.

We ran the wall again, for about a half hour, but the result was the same. That was enough for the day. The sun would be in a more cooperative position in the morning.

Torro and Ramon reluctantly decided to make a camp close by, so that they had eyes on the gringos. It was a nasty, uncomfortable night on the edge of the jungle what with the mosquitoes and gnats, and much worse things, wandering about, but they survived it. Money is one of the top-three motivators. Sex and power are probably the other two. Patriotism, faith, and love used to fit into that equation. But times change…

The following day, just a little after sunrise (so we would have the benefit of the sunlight against the walls), Will and I were in the air again.

It was on the fifth pass, when I had pulled away a little, that I heard Will grunt, then point. "Shit!" he exclaimed. "Son of a bitch! I think I saw it! The face! The face! Swing around, do it again!"

Sure enough, on the next pass, at just the right angle and just the right height, there certainly seemed to be a face. The image appeared, spread out over perhaps fifty yards, then disappeared as we soared by. Even then, it looked a good deal like a natural phenomenon. Those rock cliffs had been punished by a couple of centuries of wind and weather. It took us another three passes to nail it down, and get a location on the "right eye." Then we had to determine landmarks on the top of the ridge that correlated to the "eye" below, which was still a good hundred feet down the face of the cliff.

We had Travis and Cody, and the kids, of course, spread out along the top of the cliff as we made pass after pass. Using two-way radios, finally, we had Cody standing on the ridge exactly above the "cave." Our friends marked the spot. Tomorrow, we'd rappel down to what we hoped was an opening and not an optical illusion. It was all somewhat of a task, and by the end of the day, we were all exhausted. But we were also bloody-well excited.

The truth was, the average person would never have seen a face there, let alone an eye. You had to know what you were looking for, and you had to have more luck than you deserved. But luck was one of our strong points.

Unfortunately, there was some good and some bad in the luck business that day. In the jungle behind the camp sat the Smithsonian's Bill Simpson and two of his men. They recognized that there appeared to have been some success that day.

Simpson had chartered a plane out of Key West on the Smithsonian's dollar, and he and his team had come into Caracas International a day after the group in the Keys had landed. He had tapped a phone on one of the team members a few days before, and had the information on "this archaeological outlaw bunch" from Key West, and their plans, well before they departed for Venezuela. Admittedly, it was a little hazy — something to do with a crystal skull, of course, and possibly a cave somewhere that his boss, Thomason, wanted covered. The conversations they had taped were about returning to the cliffs where the base-jumping contest had been held — to the airfield there. The plan was pretty clear — rent a four-wheel vehicle, drive up the coast to the backside of the mountain in question, then crawl their way up the dirt road to the cliffs/airstrip, and dig in.

"Wait…watch them…and if they find something of importance, take it by whatever means necessary. If you can't hold on to it, destroy it," Thomason had said. "Given the state of affairs now, what the world doesn't know about, it doesn't need. And a freaking crystal skull that communicates in any fashion is high on that list. Am I clear?"

Thomason hung up the phone that day and exhaled hard. He thought about that dammed creepy skull they had in the basement and shivered. *The damned thing asked him questions…once…in his head… Freaking thing should be put in a company trash compactor and the pieces tossed into the ocean…*

About the same time, no more than a couple hundred yards to the east of the Smithsonian's people, the two mountain bandits were hunkered down at the periphery of the jungle, waiting, watching — well aware now of all the players in this drama.

Like Rufus had mentioned on occasion — *"Da gods, dey not often content with 'simple.' Dere be no fun in simple…"*

And in this case, he was right. You needed a bloody scorecard to keep the players straight.

CHAPTER THIRTEEN

At sunup the following day, we were gathering gear and packing ropes and markers with securing rods for the ground at the top of the cliff. Everyone was chomping at the bit to be part of the vanguard into that cave (if there was an actual cave and not just a well-worn indentation) but unfortunately, I was probably the lightest of the group (with the exception of Jing) and after seeing the opening, I realized this effort required a good deal of strength. Besides, I had some idea of what we were looking for. So, I was chosen to go.

As I leaned over the edge, that simple nylon cord around my waist being the only thing between me and an ugly dirt-smack a thousand feet below, I wasn't so sure I'd done myself a favor. One look at Will above me, grasping the rope, and I was certain he understood.

"Take it...to the limit..." he whispered.

I offered a shaky smile and began my descent, my team above me easing out the rope.

The sun had cleared the horizon in the east and the wind had come up a little. My hands were already sweating in my leather gloves, and my heavy laced boots (which we had brought for this occasion), felt bulky and cumbersome. Gradually, my friends let the rope out, dropping me slowly, while I tried not to look at the dizzy panorama below. Instead, I watched for "the eye" in the rock that should be about another hundred feet down.

Gradually, I worked my way along the rough rock wall (my only connection to *terra firma*), constantly scanning, straining to push myself out on occasion in hopes of glimpsing a cave to one side or the other. Oddly enough, Jing's hawk had chosen to accompany me, soaring along the wall of the cliff above and below me like a sentinel or a benevolent spirit. It was odd, but encouraging, as if perhaps the creature saw more than I did, or was trying to protect me.

We were nearly out of rope and I was nearly out of courage, when suddenly, I saw it — a ragged hole in the wall. Definitely a wind- and rain-worn orifice about four feet by four feet. Nature had punished the opening for so long that it lacked a defining shape and its location made it all but invisible to anything but birds.

"I've got something! To my right a little — an opening..." I cried, my voice high with tension (and a good deal of sensible fear).

There was a pause for a few moments while my people took stock of our good fortune with cheers and hugs.

"Hey! Remember me?" I yelled. "The guy on the rope?"

"Okay, okay," called Travis. "We're going to move you over a little. Don't pee your pants. You're in the process of impressing me right now."

I have to admit, Travis wasn't far from wrong. I was never good with heights, and this was just bloody-well crazy shit. But damn, I had to see what was in that cave!

Five minutes later, after a good deal of grunting from the team above, matched by my imitation of a terrified lizard, I was staring into the gloomy dark, spider-webbed mouth of the cave. The entrance was just large enough for a big man to get through comfortably. *This was not one of those things you could put off and still keep your seat at the special table at Eddie's.*

I brushed away the spiders, reached out, and pulled myself in. Sitting against the wall for a minute or two, I caught my breath, then reached down and pulled out my flashlight. Pointing it inside, I slowly moved the beam about. The cave appeared to be no more than fifteen by twenty feet, with maybe a five-foot ceiling. I had to hunch over a little to move about comfortably. I would have guessed it was man-made but I wasn't sure. Given what I knew geologically about this coastline, it would have to have been done hundreds of years ago. Maybe more...

For the next couple of hours we worked in shifts, helping members of the team make their way down to the cave for a look and some excavation. Tax and Jing were fascinated with the possibility of discovery, but they were young and quickly grew bored with the cave. We ran a metal detector across it, then dug up the few inches of accumulated dirt on the floor from one end of the cave to the other. It was a lot of effort for pretty much nothing.

In the end, the kids, Travis, and Cody made their way back to the top of the cliff. Will sat against the rock wall of the cave with

Rinco, who smoked a cigarette. I was standing just inside the entrance. The sun was slipping toward the horizon and we were catching some of its rays through the opening of the cave.

"Well, my friends," I said. "I'm as reluctant to give up as you are, but I think it's time to go. Whatever secrets this place has, it's going to keep today."

"Too true, mon," said Rinco. "Just finishing my smoke..."

I sighed and leaned back against the wall, but when I did, I caught a glimpse of something at the back of the cave. The sinking sun had captured a glint at the base of the rough stone. I didn't move. I thought it was the sun playing me, or probably just touching some mica in the rock. But it held for a few moments, and as the sun moved into it, the spot grew brighter. Then it faded.

I was going to let it go. It had been a long day. But Rinco spoke up. "Did you see that, man? That...sparkle...for a moment?"

"What sparkle?" asked Will, next to him.

"I saw it," I replied. "But it's gone now... But it was ...strange," I muttered, straightening up. My feet were already moving. A moment later, I was standing by the wall in the back, running my hands over the rock. I would have sworn I heard a voice in my head. *Here...* it said. *Here...*

I hardly noticed as I started to run my hands across the stone. Rinco and Will were there beside me now, kneeling in front of the wall, running their hands over the stone as well. I heard the words again. *Here... Here...* Suddenly, I felt like I had brushed something much larger than me. It was very spooky. My first thought was, *This would be a good time to crawl out of this hole in the wall and return to the real world.* But Will and Rinco were already pulling at the cleverly disguised, softly mortared stones. I don't remember when exactly, but I do know that a few moments later, there appeared a skull — a crystal clear, detailed, magnificently cut, human-sized skull, staring at us from a carved rock enclave of sorts.

I reached out hesitantly — I knew it probably wasn't the wisest of things to do right away, but I did it and I don't know why — and touched the crystal skull.

Suddenly, in my mind, it was as if there was a wind swirling around me, and a great rush or movement, but not in the physical sense, and for a moment, I couldn't see. Then I found myself in a

126

sterile hospital room, and there I saw my old girlfriend (well, mine and Will's old girlfriend, Banyan McDaniels), giving birth to my son in the Barbados Island hospital...twenty-three years ago. I had no idea he even existed at that time. But later, it was one of the things I regretted most in my life — that I hadn't been there for that moment, when he came into the world... That it wasn't my face he saw first, and my hands he felt touch him and hold him. It was a hugely important possession that I had wanted so much to carry with me but it was a gift I could never have had...until this moment. I picked him up. He was wrapped in a warm blanket. I felt his tiny hands in mine, I saw his eyes clear and come alive with life, and I suddenly felt a peace and a joy that I never knew existed. It was as if...it knew...the skull knew what to give me.

As I stepped back, stunned by my revelations, Rinco was drawn in. He reached down and touched the skull. His eyes went wide, then softened and he stood there like a statue, his countenance distant. A few moments later, tears were running down his cheeks but he was smiling. Finally, he stepped back and Will was the last to be drawn in. He reached down and picked up the skull, and for a moment, there was the strangest look on his face, then it melted into surprise, and morphed into the most pleasant joy. When he finally set it down and pulled away, he exhaled softly and smiled, and there was a rare serenity about my friend.

Rinco looked at us and sighed, his face more at peace than I could remember ever seeing. "I don't know about you guys...but I just had the most remarkable experience," he whispered. "I don't know what else to call it." Our friend sighed softly, his eyes distant but remarkably content. He shook his head, tears still running down his face. "I just saw my dog, Custer — my partner in Afghanistan. He was happy and...whole...and he was waiting for me." Rinco drew a shaky breath and let it out. "He's okay...and good...and he's there, on the other side..."

Will offered a remarkably content smile. "I just saw the woman I'm going to marry," he whispered, with a small amount of incredulousness. "Not too far from now. She's pretty and she's kind, and for some damned reason, she's gonna love me." Then my friend smiled, more at ease than I had seen for quite a while. "And she's just around the corner of my future..." He grinned. "Can you imagine?"

That was an equally stunning "prophecy."

It seemed as if the skull responded intuitively to what you were, and that's where the pride or the peace or the pain came in. I had an intuitive suspicion that folks like serial killers or habitual liars would not find their experience so pleasant with that crafted piece of crystal, if they were allowed anything at all. It showed you the deepest parts of you — good or bad. It took them out and danced with them.

We had discovered what we'd set out to find — which seemed nearly impossible. Even more remarkable were the "connections" to the skull that a few of us had experienced. But now, as we decided to wrap up our find and take it with us, the crystal face seemed to become stoic and quiet, and the power within it seemed to have withdrawn. I put it in a velour sack I brought and stuffed it into my backpack.

As we entered our camp, it was the last of the evening, and the shadows were stretching out and absorbing the life around them. We were all physically and mentally weary. It had been an extraordinary day. Not only had we found the object of our search far easier than anyone expected, but we now realized (that is to say, a *few of us* realized) the width and depth of this remarkable object. After what I had experienced, I was forced to accept the possibility of greater forces than this simple, arrogant amalgam called man. The real questions now were who or what, and from where? I took the skull and put it in Cody's Cessna, on the floor of the front seat, and covered it with a towel.

After a simple dinner, we sat around the campfire, the dark sky blanketing us, filled with a million brilliant stars. No one said the words but it was almost as if something wasn't complete... Like somebody had left an important message on the answering machine that I hadn't heard. It was really weird.

Will, who had been profoundly affected by all that had taken place, poked at the fire with a stick. As the glowing embers danced up, joining the stars, Will eased out a breath and glanced around at all of us, then spoke quietly. "This whole affair has really reinforced my personal perspective. Basically, I was raised as a 'meat and potatoes' guy when it came to religion and all that goes with it.

Conventional is the word that comes to mind. But…spending so much time in 'mind-expanding' adventures…" He nodded at me. "…has changed my view of things. And now, this discovery…" My buddy took a breath, exhaled heavily again, and continued.

"I know this is far and away, but with what has happened here today to me and my friends — from what we've discovered and experienced — I'm struck by the distinct conclusion that there must be other…*folks*…out there." He pointed up at the dark, starlit sky, then turned back to us. "What we have discovered is simply not of this world. We don't have anything like it. The science, the mechanics, are way beyond anything we have. It had to come from elsewhere. Really, when you think about it, why wouldn't it be possible — with all the billions of solar systems in an apparently never-ending universe? Why wouldn't God have created an additional intelligent species or two here and there?" Will shrugged. "Yeah, I know what the Bible says. We're the one and only. But I sometimes think we need to bear in mind that while God may be all-knowing and flawless, the people who copied the original Bible by hand, then recopied, then interpreted it in secular councils, then recopied it again for hundreds of years after Jesus' death, were human…and they had issues."

My friend sighed. "I'm just saying, why all the effort to create 'intelligent life' on only one small, fragile, continually rupturing ball of dirt and water, and nowhere else in a never-ending universe while nurturing a species, that at best, is its own worst enemy, and is certainly the nemesis of just about anything it comes into contact with. My impression of God is, He's a bigger thinker than that."

Our friend took a breath. He was on a roll. "What if there *were* benign intergalactic travelers — celestial missionaries of sorts — from other, highly advanced civilizations? What if a few of these… galactic emissaries…were far enough advanced to have genuine communication with Spirit?" He paused and held out his arms. "Isn't that exactly what the holy men throughout our planet's history claimed they could do? Jesus, Buddha, Confucius? Talk to God? And have Him answer? Huh?" He paused and stared at us. "If you buy one, you've opened yourself to the other. I'm talking about the possibility of a basically humanoid species that believed in, and perhaps worked in conjunction with, the higher power of Spirit and who occasionally 'nudged' or 'preserved' particular enclaves of spirit-divined intelligent life — groups who represented a significant advancement for their particular planet. And maybe they used devices like this remarkable skull to deliver their messages telepathically."

Again my friend drew a breath and glanced around. "There are several similar instances in the Bible of Spirit communicating with people — usually to guide them or get them out of a bad situation." He smiled. "Miracles, I think they were called."

Will exhaled, slightly embarrassed by his dissertation. "I'm not saying I'm dead right about any of this, by any means, and I won't fall into the trap of theological presumption that's twisted mankind's common sense for thousands of years. I'm just saying..." He smiled. "I'll leave you with an expression by our buddy, Rufus. *'Remember, mon, a miracle is jus' a good thing we don' understand.'*"

Strangely enough, it was Rinco who spoke next. He offered a short sigh. "Everyone needs something to believe in. But the problem is, we're herd animals, taking succor in being part of the herd, and most often carrying disdain for the other herds/tribes, and distrust for those who don't join our tribe. Politics and religion were originally supposed to help us find spiritual peace and social organization, if not comfort. But let's face it, organized religion and politics have terrible track records, perpetually razing entire cultures that didn't agree with their philosophy." Our friend took a breath and sighed again. "The worst part is, it's always a small handful of blindly greedy, conscience-challenged assholes that determine who the heretics, political or religious, are."

Damned if he wasn't right.

Rinco turned to me. "What's your take on this...crystal head? You seem to have the best connection. You found it."

I shrugged. "I don't really know but if I had to guess, I'd say it's some sort of highly intuitive, exotic computer, perhaps drawing energy in an ethereal fashion and projecting information telepathically. The more we have come to learn, the more we know that thoughts carry energy — bad and good. And possibly it can draw from the persona and physical history of a person or even a group of persons, like a tribe or a culture... Then control at least partially what takes place by seeing ahead and behind. I would bet that once you got comfortable with that, you could ask it questions and get answers." I paused. "But I wouldn't be surprised if it intuitively weighs the individual or individuals asking questions. A few people would get answers, but for most people, especially nowadays, it would just be a crystal head."

"True dat..." mumbled Tax.

"That would be a handy gadget," said Travis, who had been silent through much of this. "What a gift for a young culture or civilization."

While we were in the process of moderate revelations, we would have been less enthusiastic if we had known about the plans being made for us...

"It be time for some pay-backing here," muttered Torro in Spanish as he ran a hand across his face, annoying the mosquitoes. "They found the head! The spooky head! I watch 'em pull it out of the bag and look at it, then put it in the big plane!"

"We wait till they go to sleep," said his friend. "Then we go in and get it..."

It was summer and it was warm — way too warm to sleep in the aircraft, even though that would have helped with the mosquitoes and safety — so we spread out our bedrolls around the campfire. We drew straws for the first guard duty. Tax lost. It was okay, he was young and sleep wasn't quite as important. It wasn't long and the rest of us were asleep. It had been a challenging day.

"Wake up, Carle, wake up," hissed Ramon as he shook his partner in mostly unsuccessful crimes at the edge of the jungle. "Time to steal a head. While you rest, I do some scouting. This seems like a very popular place for *gringos* now. There be another bunch, three of them, in the jungle to the east."

"Torro..." murmured his friend as he blinked a few times and waved off a persistent mosquito. "My name...is Torro..." He exhaled, his eyes cleared, and he glared at his friend. "When you die, I'm gonna have them bury you upside down in the ground with a banana in your butt!" The little Venezuelan looked around. The moon through the trees was nearly high. "Yeah," he muttered. "Time to go steal a head…" He blinked a few more times and grinned. "Probably not as much fun as 'getting some head,' but more profitable…"

The plan for the two banditos in residence was pretty straightforward. The level of intellect here didn't allow for too much in the way of mental gymnastics. Just slip in, pick the lock on the airplane door, and steal the skull. No leaving a rose or a coin or any "Hi-Ho Silvers" in the distance. These guys were "meat and potatoes" bandits.

The first part of their plan went better than even they expected. Tax had taken a walk to the edge of the cliff to view the moon and the ocean. Everyone else was asleep, and the lock on the plane door turned out to be a simple challenge for Ramon. Things were looking good. They reached into the aircraft and grabbed the head (which was in a velour bag), and started out, moving around the backside of the plane so as to not draw attention. All good…

That was when they stepped on the canvas sheet hiding the already somewhat smelly, deep latrine that Tax had dug.

We all awoke to a surprised yelp and someone yelling about "stinkin' like chit!"

Most of us arrived just as our old bandito friends were pulling themselves out of our latrine. It was truly foul play. Mucking mischief…

The little guy dragged himself out and spun around dramatically as he faced us. He held up a forefinger. "You are in son serious trouble, gringos. I an a very bad bandito — one of de baddest…" The finger came up again. "I'ne so bad —"

"You're so bad, you stink…" groaned Will, remembering these two guys from our last Venezuelan experience.

Behind Torro stood his friend, holding the bag, you might say, which seemed to remain mostly unmucked, thank goodness. (The pit was a recent creation but it doesn't take too long for several big men to foul a four-by-four hole.)

Torro straightened and regained some composure. He offered a cocky smile. "If you let us go, we won't tell anybody that chu found dat crystal head."

That surprised us but Will countered nicely. "If we push you off the cliff, you won't tell anyone anything."

That got their attention.

"We're going to be out of here tomorrow, anyway," I added.

"Shit!" spat the little bandit. "I'n not getting no head anywhere in dis!" But Torro got that cocky look again. "If I tell you sonthing berry, berry important, maybe you jus' let us ride off into de sunset, huh?"

"Depends on how important," replied Travis.

Torro exhaled and wagged a finger at us. "Chu got son other gringos just arrivin' here — dey come in a jeep, aroun' da back of da mountain... Dey look like dey belong in da city — not happy in da jungle...and dey got guns." He pointed. "Over dere."

Travis looked at Cody. His friend nodded. "Sounds like a fair trade to me." He stared at the two banditos. "Okay, get out of here. You come back, we push you off the cliff."

Cody exhaled heavily as the Laurel and Hardy of bandits disappeared into the gloom of night. He cautiously peeled back the sack to make sure the skull was intact without actually touching it, then closed the bag and looked at us. "We pulled this thing out of the ground less than twenty-four hours ago and we already have people after it. Nine chances out of ten those folks in the jungle are Smithsonian heavies. How they found out about us, I don't know. It doesn't matter. The race, or the chase, is on." He shook his head sadly. "We could easily end up doing a Nikola Tesla act — trying desperately to prove our find while having all the conventional elements of science and religion doing all they can to discredit us. Or if that doesn't work, kill us."

Travis nodded. "You're right. It represents the validation of a civilization, perhaps a species, greater than our own. It will always represent a danger to conventional ecclesiastics as long as it exists. It says that there is something or someone out there equal to or greater than ourselves. And that just doesn't fly with a lot of people."

"So what do we do?" asked Will.

"I don't know," muttered Travis. "I don't know. Let's try for a little more sleep, then we get the hell out of here at dawn."

It was a good plan as far as plans go, but at dawn, as we were closing down our camp, we heard the sound of helicopters. Over the tops of the trees in the jungle came two military copters — a Bell 430 transport and a Boeing-Sikorsky RAH-66 Comanche attack helicopter — both with Venezuelan Army insignias.

The troop copter touched down and three Venezuelan soldiers stepped out while the attack copter circled above us like a hungry hawk.

As the soldiers surrounded us at a distance, an officer on a bullhorn from the helicopter announced that we were to stand down, not move. That we were in the process of breaking numerous Venezuelan antiquity laws.

We couldn't have known, but while we had been sleeping, then dealing with crazy bandits, agreements were being finalized between the Smithsonian Institution, the U.S. government, and the Venezuelan Army. Deals were made. The Smithsonian had played their backup ace. They couldn't afford to have this situation "get away from them." The Venezuelans were guaranteed one of America's newer versions of the Sikorsky-60 Blackhawk helicopters, and the U.S. government, via the Smithsonian, was guaranteed an ancient crystal skull, which, once in their possession, would never actually exist.

While we were being questioned and detained, Simpson and his people came strolling out of the foliage. The Smithsonian henchman immediately showed his identification, and with great pleasure, introduced himself to us, then took possession of the skull. Apparently, he and his team had been watching from the trees for some time, waiting for the helicopters he'd called in.

Simpson opened the bag and looked inside, then reached in and grabbed the head. A moment later, his eyes went wide, then he blanched, blinking and uneasy. Simpson tottered slightly, tilting like a tree in a heavy wind, and lost his balance, eyes now distant and way past uneasy. He dropped to his knees. Hands shaking, he quickly closed the bag, rose, and handed it to one of his people, his face pale, eyes confused, and his hands still trembling.

Will and Rinco looked at me.

"I think he just got a dose of the skull," said Rinco.

"Truth and consequences," said Will under his breath.

We were all herded over to the campfire area, guarded by two well-armed Venezuelan soldiers. After he was satisfied everything was under control, and he had regained his composure, Simpson came back to us.

"Sometimes you win, sometimes you lose," he said with a feral grin. "I'm sorry but this time, you really lose. You see, we can't let you go back to the States and start telling stories about finding a crystal skull." He glanced over at the bag, now held by one of his men. "Certainly not that damned cursed thing." He turned to Cody's 310, then back to us. "I think it's going to appear that you had problems landing here, and your plane crashed and burned...with you in it."

He smiled again. It wasn't pretty.

"I think some gasoline and a little C-4 will do the trick." Our nemesis shrugged. "I know, that's a rotten way to go, but we need some authenticity so there aren't too many questions. The Venezuelans will take care of the report." He glanced over at the skull in the bag and shivered slightly. "That bastard thing needs to disappear," he mumbled, somewhere between bitter and frightened. "Nothing should crawl inside your head like that..." He exhaled. "But right now, my boss wants to see it. After that, who knows..."

I couldn't help it. I had seen his face when he had touched it. "The skull showed you who you really are, didn't it?" I said. "Did you get a good look at yourself? Did you take a walk down memory lane?"

Simpson glared at me. I saw his hand shake as he raised it and pointed a finger at me. "Screw you, asshole! In a little while, you won't be anything but a charred memory."

"But you'll still know who you are," I replied. "You can run from yourself, but you can't hide..."

Moments later, after the soldiers had finished going through our gear, they began loading us aboard Cody's 310. I heard Jing's hawk calling to her. The eastern sky was just lightening and I made out the bird above us. Jing called out in that harsh, strange language, and the bird pulled away to the periphery of the camp. I understood, sadly. She was saving him. Keeping him away from the plane...and the coming explosion.

The few soldiers were pulling out. They were taking the Smithsonian people's four-wheel-drive Jeep off the mountain. No one wanted any witnesses here.

Simpson looked at the officer in charge. "Set the timer for fifteen minutes. I want everyone gone before this happens. No witnesses. No difference of opinions... And tell the Bell 430 pilot we'll be going out with him in his chopper. "

Our hands and feet were bound and we were shoved into the plane and tied to the standard six seats of Cody's 310. Rinco was forced into the small fold-down pony seat in the rear of the plane. There would be no proof that we were tied after the plane exploded. Like Simpson said, with his people nudging the authorities, it would just be "a bad landing that led to a fire and the destruction of the aircraft."

We sat there, bound like geese for market, and watched one of the Smithsonian guys place the explosive device and set the timer for fifteen minutes. He was out the door before the clock started ticking. A few minutes later, we heard the helicopters lifting off. Travis and Cody, tied to the pilot and copilot seats, were already struggling maniacally with their bonds, but to no avail. Not only had our limbs been bound, but we were tied to the seats as well.

From where I was, I could see the timer on the dash. Down to twelve minutes. I looked at Will, across the aisle from me. "Son of a bitch. Here we are again."

He sighed and glanced around. "But I don't see us getting out of this one."

"The good news is, it won't hurt," said Rinco behind us. "Just a flash and a bang and you're on the other side."

"And how do you know that?" grumbled Will. "You done this before?"

Rinco got a distant smile. "Yeah, I think so...somewhere..."

Travis was still lurching back and forth in his seat up front, and while he seemed to be loosening the bolts on the floor some, I didn't think he had near enough time.

Will looked at me. "Well, we've taken it to the limit one last time."

"Where's that damned miracle when you need it," muttered Cody. "Like in the movies..."

I looked over at the timer. Six minutes. I was about to answer when the door of the plane was thrown open and there stood the little bandit, Torro, and his tall buddy, behind him.

He glanced around, figuring it out quickly. Then he held up a finger and shook it at us. "Chu gonna owe me big time." He shook the finger again. "Rule number one. Neber trust da stinkin' government. I tell you dis —"

"Okay, okay!" growled Cody. "Cut the damned ropes. We'll argue social sciences later! You've got about five minutes before we all become charbroiled and well done!"

While the rest of us were getting free of our bonds, as soon as he was untied, Cody pulled himself over to the timer and examined the wiring. He found the lead wire and ran it back with his hand to the alligator clips on the main power line under the dash. We were down to about a minute when he pulled the clips and the timer stopped.

Travis, in one of his rare displays of emotion, leaned over and put his hand on his buddy's shoulder. "You're a fine man, my friend, and a good soldier, in a pinch..."

"You can buy me a drink later," replied Cody with a smile. "Right now there's this small problem of those Smithsonian bastards getting away. If I could pick them up on radar we could follow them. He hit the ignition and the instrument lights came on, as well as the radio, and things suddenly became really interesting.

A harried voice was calling in an emergency over the standard 122.2 frequency, rather than the regular emergency 122.5, obviously in a panic, almost shouting into the microphone in Spanish, then English, "Mayday! Mayday! This is Bell 430, November 77361, out of Rilo Air Force Base. We were heading west but are experiencing some sort of electrical storm...about ten miles off the coast, approximately fifteen miles east of Caracas. Instruments are gone — no readings, dark clouds closing in, lots of what looks like...lightning...engine beginning to shudder...I repeat, this is an emergency situation. Mayday... Mayday...Mayday..."

There was silence in our plane for a moment. It was not just the horror of listening to a pilot in panic mode, looking at going down in the ocean (every pilot's nightmare), but the Venezuelan coast sits on a seven-hundred to six-thousand-foot-deep basin. You don't have to be very far off shore before you're over a thousand feet of water. You lose an aircraft in that area, it's the last you're going to see of it. Even more creepy was the fact that I recognized those call numbers — that was the helicopter that had just flown away, with the Smithsonian people.

Will said the words. "That was Simpson's helicopter — the Smithsonian guys…and the skull…"

We waited for well over a half hour, listening to the plane radio and the search-and-rescue units. There was lots of chatter and speculation, but the bottom line was, the helicopter was gone. No radar signal, no radio response, no oil slicks, no nothing at this point. It was as if it had just disappeared. Again, the big problem in terms of search and rescue was the deep basin and the unusual heavy weather pattern that had suddenly appeared, and was now dissipating.

The truth was, that's what I wanted to think was the problem. The other scenario just freaked me out too badly.

Maybe someone decided they didn't want anyone having that skull…

CHAPTER FOURTEEN

There was little left for us to do. We didn't want to be found at the point of departure for the lost aircraft — too many questions there — so we gathered our gear, buckled up, and headed back to Caracas for the night, sticking very tightly to the coastline. Before leaving, we all chipped in and came up with six hundred American dollars for Torro and his partner in crime, which made them relatively happy bandits.

Throughout the evening and into the following morning, we followed the news on the "aircraft disappearance." None of it was good. At this point, the authorities were calling it a possible catastrophic engine failure or a lightning strike. There was no recovery of any wreckage or personnel.

"Could someone or something out there actually have orchestrated this?" Will asked as we sat around a quiet breakfast in the hotel restaurant in the morning.

"Could just as easily have been one of the storms this area is known for," said Travis, trying to bring us back to earth.

"I don't think we'll ever know," I said. "The only thing we can carry out of this is, and I'm quoting Shakespeare: *There are more things in heaven and earth, Horatio, than are dreamt of in your philosophy...*"

Jing, who had been quiet through much of this but was obviously moved, whispered, "I'm reminded that a government big enough to give you everything you want is big enough to take anything they want..." She exhaled. "We need to be getting out of here pretty soon."

As we were finishing up, Travis looked around at us. "I agree with Jing but...while we're here, maybe we ought to check in with the authorities again. Just to see if there's any fresh news on Eddie..." He sighed, knowing he was chasing butterflies. "We can check with the Department of the Interior again, here in Caracas, and there are a couple of trading companies that supply goods for people who trade in the interior — like that river fellow that we saved. What was his name...Silvano Petros! That was it."

The rest of us nodded.

"Can't hurt," muttered Will. But he sighed, more resigned than confident. "Confucius once said, 'the definition of futility is looking for a black cat in a dark room.' But what the hell, maybe we'll step on his tail."

As it turned out, the officer in charge of Venezuela's Department of the Interior said he had been trying to reach us on the number we had left (Travis's home phone) but he hadn't gotten a reply. Evidently, he'd started calling just about the time we were leaving for Venezuela. We'd been busy following crystal skulls, river pirates, Caracas banditos, and being chased by the Smithsonian, and no one was checking answering machines once we got to the other side of the big pond.

The information was spotty at best and probably second or third hand. Basically, an old river trader (much like the fellow Silvano Petros) had heard the Indians way up the Maracao River and deep into the Amazon jungle talk about finding a white man. They were a hunting party from a tribe way south. Instead of carrying the barely alive man north, toward civilization, they continued on their way home. The story was, they sold him to a village deep into the Amazon jungle — *una mujeres de la selva.*

Will flashed me a look. *Mujeres de la selva...* jungle women. That sounded nastily familiar.

The fellow paused. "As the story goes, he was apparently pretty banged up. The people who found him didn't have the means to take care of him and thought he was going to die. The village they sold him to agreed to care for him."

"Holy shit!" said Will. "Not the damned village of women thing again!"

I turned to my friend. "If you remember, the 'girls of our dreams' told us there was another village like them, much farther south."

"How do we find them?" asked Travis. "How do we find this village of Amazons?"

The guy shrugged. "The only thing the man mentioned about the place was that it was on a tiny tributary just off a main river, off the Maracaibo. The tributary curled off like a fishing hook, and the mound was in the center of the hook." He thought for a moment, then raised a finger. "Nobody goes back that far, except natives — nothing but muddy water, dense jungle, and things that want to eat you. But he said he was told there was a hill that the village was built on — sort of a geological anomaly that rose out of the jungle like a mole, maybe three hundred yards wide. The natives had landscaped that and built their huts there." He glanced around at us. "That should stand out from the air." He paused and dropped into his official guide voice. "Fifty percent of Venezuela's area is composed of forested land, including 18 million hectares of Amazon rainforest in the southern state of Amazonas. It's easy for entire tribes to be uncounted in the larger picture..." He paused then and smiled. "But that hump off the Maracaibo should stand out from the air. I'll mark a map now, with some easily visible landmarks, to keep you on track." Then he paused again. "But that's serious jungle back in there. Only a couple big rivers. The rest is a huge spider's web of tiny waterways. Very difficult to get into, very easy to get lost."

"Son of a bitch," Will huffed, undaunted, as he looked at us. "Eddie might actually be alive! Damn, that's some incredible news!"

"Okay team," Travis said. "Let's not lose sight of the fact that the odds are not good here." Then he smiled. "But at least we have odds now. Time to saddle up again." He turned to me. "We'll take your floatplane — gives us the best chance to find a place to get down on a waterway and into the jungle."

It was a sliver of hope. The story could be exaggerated or an outright lie, and Eddie might not have survived the trauma of the crash or it might not be Eddie at all. On top of that, we might not even be able to find what we were looking for. It was the middle of the damned Amazon jungle, for God's sake, the biggest piece of greenery in the world.

It didn't matter. We'd be going after our friend if he were in the arms of the devil himself and in the center of Hell. It didn't matter. We returned to our hotel and laid some plans.

My 182 wasn't designed, interior or weight limitations-wise, for seven people, and then there was Eddie, if we found him. It was a tough call, but Tax, Jing, and Rinco agreed to sit this ride out. Even then, with Eddie (if we got that lucky), who was a fairly sizeable guy, and the fuel needed, it could be touch and go, depending on the river. This was way back into the Amazon — a place with "no love," as Rinco put it.

As far as the weight issue, I figured if I alternately "rocked" the pontoons back and forth off the water a little on takeoff to break the bond with the surface, we'd probably make it. We put together a little "just in case package" — some foodstuffs, a couple of portable radios, mosquito nets, and the medical box from Cody's 310.

It was a long night of conjecture and hope. It was hard to believe we had a chance at this, after believing for so long that our friend was gone.

We were out at dawn the following day.

The good news was, the Department of the Interior officer had offered solid directions — particularly about the partially cleared mound coming up out of the jungle with the settlement, which we found relatively easily, although we noticed several of those before we got to our destination. The bad news was the density of the jungle and the narrow creeks coming off the river that accessed the mound. We did a couple of pass-overs but didn't see much — just a bunch of women staring up at us as we sailed by. But on the last pass, it seemed like I saw a man step out from one of the huts. His hair was long and hid his face and he moved with a pronounced limp, but damn, he did look a little familiar.

To get into this jungle hamlet we would be forced to land back on the river, several hundred yards from the knoll, and take one of the foot trails that led from the river to the village. There were a couple of drawbacks there. First off, it was a more dangerous way of doing things. If something went wrong, there was less chance of us escaping. I mean, it was possible, just a little tricky. It was probably a quarter-mile from the village to the river.

"I think maybe we ought to try something," said Will. "Let's do a pass-over and drop one of our portable VHF radios. If that was a guy down there — a white man, maybe Eddie...he'll pick it up."

It was a good plan, to a point.

We made the pass, and when we saw the guy, Will dropped the radio, wrapped in a survival blanket. I swung back around in a tight loop, circled, and watched as the fellow limped over, picked up the package, and found the radio.

Will brought up our radio. "This is Will Bell, originally from Key West, Florida. If you can hear me, come back by pressing the intercom button on the side of the radio and holding it while you speak, then releasing while you listen for a response."

As I brought us back around in a tight turn, a voice came back over the radio — a gravelly voice with a Southern hippie dialect. "*Hola*, dude, *hola*. Are you in trouble? Can I help you?"

We glanced at each other. We all recognized that voice.

"Son of a bitch!" muttered an incredulous Cody from the back. "It's him! It's Eddie!"

We were giggling crazy for a few moments, then Will composed himself and responded. "Jesus! No, man," he yelled. "We're not in trouble. We want to help you! This is Will Bell, your old friend, and I'm with Kansas and Cody and Travis!"

There was a heavy pause. "Sorry, man, but I don't recognize any of those dudes," the fellow below replied slowly, as if he was weighing what he'd just heard. "I mean, man, the names are sort of familiar, but..."

"For God's sake, Eddie, we've come to take you home!" Will cried again. "This is Will! Will Bell! From the Florida Keys!"

There was another long silence. "Sorry, man, I don't know you, I don't think. But then I did have an accident...something about an airplane I think, but I can't remember exactly. I banged my head...and other parts, hard. These fine ladies in this village found me and sort of nursed me back to health. Very strange...all women...and the women, man, you just can't imagine how friendly they are."

Will immediately jerked around to me, his eyes speaking what I was thinking. *They said there was another village far south in the jungle that had the same inclination regarding singular gender and...pollination... Our amorous companions from the crazy horny village told us that!*

"Jesus! I hate coincidences!" I growled, glancing back at Will. "I freaking hate 'em!"

While I kept us in a tight circle above the village — women coming out of the huts now, staring upward at us, hands shading their eyes — *but no men* — Eddie continued. "Man, I appreciate your concern, but except for this memory slippage thing, dude, I'm a pretty happy camper. I mean, good food, and they got this great fruit punch they give me every day — makes me sort of...groovy... and I get horny as a badger. And they're real accommodating about that." He chuckled. "And they've been telling me about a sort of ceremony coming up where I'm gonna be the guest of honor. Man, you're not gonna believe this," he whispered into the radio. "But it's sort of a screw till you drop kind of thing, for a day or so. Can you dig it, dude, I mean, what a gig, huh? Is that far out or what?"

"Eddie, listen..."

"Dude," my friend interrupted. "I admit this Eddie guy sounds vaguely familiar but man, my name is Kahuga...they tell me. And I don't care if my name is Eddie or Charley or Uncle Ben. I don't wanna be rescued. You dig? I mean, like, this is a very copasetic gig and I don't want to blow it."

He talked like Eddie, he sounded like Eddie, he even looked like a roughed-up version of Eddie, but the boy did not want to be saved. And that was a problem because there was no question that our boy was gonna get served up on a platter to the god of procreation.

"I may not want to stay here for the rest of my life," Eddie continued. "But I gotta tell you, dude, I be a pretty content guy — I mean man, can you imagine a gig like this? It's like being king of your own little space — damned near every man's dream."

Sure, it's every man's dream — if they don't plan on killing you after the big party!

I glanced around at my friends, and Will, as he did so often, read my thoughts.

"We're going to have to do an intervention here. We gotta get that stupid horny son of a bitch out of there before they drug him up, drain him dry, and cut his throat, all the while singing *Kumbaya*." Will practically yelled into the mike, glaring at it as if it were an animate creature. "Listen, Eddie, listen to me! If you value your dick and your life, you will do exactly what I say. You get the hell out of there tonight, when everyone's sleeping, and you run for the river as fast as your skinny legs will allow you to. Do you understand? We'll be waiting. There's a full moon. You'll see the floatplane as you come to the river."

I could hear Eddie sigh. "Kahuga, dude...my name is Kahuga, and no, man, I think you got the wrong guy, wrong gig. I mean, I've never been around a more…accommodating, if not generous group of ladies… It's like being king, dude." He chuckled. "My people love me!"

Will looked around at us, flustered and clearly frightened for our friend. "Yeah…they love you…then they don't…"

I turned back to Will and our eyes met. "We gotta make a new plan, Stan."

My friend offered a bitter smile. "Get him out the back, Jack…"

CHAPTER FIFTEEN

There was no point in all of us going in to get our muddled friend. Too many people would turn this into a serious fracas and none of us wanted to tangle with a village of crazy-assed, horny women. This had to be subtle, if Eddie cooperated. It was going to get less than subtle if he didn't. We were bringing our boy home, whether he wanted it or not.

We all piled into my floatplane and flew away. A few minutes later, we landed on the river about five miles out and sat for an hour. The sun was well past its zenith and moving toward the horizon. After a while, we motored back on the surface, keeping the engine just above idle, running quietly, like a boat. It was almost dark by the time we found the creek that wound its way to the village. We moved out onto the pontoons and began paddling, using the folding emergency paddles stored in the stern compartment. When we were about a hundred yards from the village, we swung the plane around, facing outward, downriver — always a smart thing to do when you might have to make a hasty getaway. We then tied her to the mangroves.

There was a trail. We waited for the moon to rise. It was full and bright, casting a glow that seemed almost like daytime.

Finally, Travis glanced around, then nodded to us all. "Time to go," he said.

Will was chosen to watch the plane. He flew well and could handle "first seat" and getting us out if we were in a hurry.

With the yellow moon on our shoulders, Travis, Cody, and I moved like wraiths. The village was smaller than the one Will and I had dealt with before, which was good, and everyone appeared to be tucked away for the night. The last, fragrant smoke from dying cooking fires drifted in gossamer sheets across the camp. There didn't appear to be any night sentinels. We crept in, silent as ghosts, wary as cats. I remembered the hut I saw Eddie step out of earlier that afternoon as we flew over. That seemed like the place to start.

Quietly, staying with the perimeter, we worked our way around to the hut and onto its deck. I pulled back the cloth curtain/door.

There was Eddie, sleeping on a floor mat, by himself, thank goodness. We all crouched around our friend, then I gently shook him. His one eye opened and he blinked a few times, then turned and looked at us. His eye widened and I thought he recognized us. Then he spoke.

"I don't know who you guys are or what you want, but you're going to have to find your own huts. This one's mine."

At that point, Travis moved in a little and pointed up at the ceiling with his left hand. When Eddie reflexively looked up, Travis clipped him solidly on the jaw with a right. Our "lost but found" friend dropped like a sack of flour. Travis grabbed Eddie by one hand and effortlessly pulled him up and over his shoulder. "Time to go, gentlemen," he growled.

It had all gone remarkably well, and I always get nervous when that happens because like our Rastaman friend always says, *"The gods, they don' like simple — dere be no entertainment in it."*

We were creeping along the edge of the village toward the path that led back to the plane, when one of the women stepped out of her hut to relieve herself. She had just squatted at the back when she saw us carrying away her scheduled entertainment.

The woman bellowed out a warning. I thought about trying to calm her since she was only a few yards away…but generally, trying to calm an agitated woman works about as well as trying to baptize a cat. And we had a group of angry women here, with bows and arrows and knives. Not good…

Fortunately, we had a bit of a lead. It took the villagers a couple of minutes to figure out what had happened.

As we ran for the trail that would take us back to the plane, I pulled out my portable VHF phone. "Will! Will, comeback! We've got problems. We got Eddie but the better part of the tribe is after us. We're gonna need one of your famous diversions. Pretty quick! Something to get their attention, dude!"

Will stood there in the jungle by the plane, bathed by a slice of moonlight, listening to my frantic warning. He had less than ten minutes to come up with an attention-getter. My friend, suddenly sweating, was trying desperately to figure out what he could do to stop an angry horde of women, short of shooting somebody (which could easily become an international incident — *"Americans fly into*

Venezuelan jungle and shoot natives for sport."). He looked around, stopping at the plane. He thought for a moment, then got one of those sly smiles. Diversions were really his specialty. *Something that wouldn't kill anyone but would stop the show...*

He ran to the plane and pulled out the small, boombox/tape deck that Tax and Jing carried with them everywhere. They were young — they needed music like they needed water. Will frantically dug through their box of tapes, then smiled and grabbed one. My friend realized this diversion had to strike the right nerves. He was dealing with a group of horny, now angry women. There's nothing that gets more attention than sex and religion.

Next, Will stumbled to the airplane equipment and supply box in the back of the storage compartment and found a can of yellow grease used for the wheel bearings. He stripped to absolutely nothing and rubbed the grease all over his body. In a few moments, he was a startling soft yellow from head to foot. From there the plan went to "rated X." He grabbed some eye shadow from a makeup kit that Jing had left in the plane, and gave himself some fairly spooky eyes, somewhere between Rudolph Valentino and Beelzebub. To top it off, Will was one of those guys that was, let's say, remarkably well-endowed — very hard to compete with on our occasional sexual forays with girls who liked occasional collective entertainment. His nickname in college was "Donkey Boy."

We came stumbling in, partly carrying, partly dragging an awake but somewhat reluctant Eddie. The natives were seriously restless and not too far behind us. They weren't at all happy about losing their upcoming entertainment. They may have wanted blood before, but that was after sex. All they wanted now was blood.

We all screeched to a halt as Will came out from around the plane looking like something out of a bad Halloween porno flick.

"What the hell?" said Travis. "What..."

"Don't ask," cried Will. "Just get in the plane and get her fired up. I'm going to try and hold them while you get ready."

"Hold them with what?" muttered Cody. "A porno show?"

Will nodded. "Yeah, sort of. It came to me that many of the cultures of the Amazon basin — at least the Indian ones — worship sexual deities." He smiled. "We only have two choices — we shoot a bunch of women and risk a major incident, or we appeal to their baser instincts." He grinned. "Especially this tribe."

We scrambled into the airplane and I did a quick run-up as the natives arrived and Will went into the performance of a lifetime. My friend's Spanish was good, and that seemed to be the nexus of most of the tribal languages. He gambled on that and won the roll. But the truth was, a lot of this show was more...visual.

As the women poured into the clearing, panting, angry, and armed, my naked buddy magically appeared from behind a tree, threw his arms out and spread his legs (which gave good definition to his...act...) "I am the god of hellfire! And hot sex!" he shouted, arms out like he was parting the Red Sea. "I come to you from the netherworld of Jumping Bones...to satisfy your needs! To feed the kitty! To fill your wombs with rug rats and knee-biters!"

He did an impressive hip thrust. There was significant gasping and wide eyes, and the audience fell back slightly. One woman lost her balance and had to be helped up.

Will took advantage of the gained ground. "Return to your village and await me! We will soon do the four-legged frolic!"

There was some hesitation, partly because they weren't sure if he was for real and partly because they couldn't pull their eyes away from Will's...act. An arrow zinged out and stuck in the tree trunk by him, but somehow my friend maintained his composure. It shook him but he manned up, threw out his hands, and did another hip thrust. Another girl collapsed into the arms of her friends.

"I, the god of the horizontal mambo, comes to you tonight — to plant my seed among you!" he cried.

Will did a little "snake toss" on the word "seed" and another woman moaned, sinking to her knees. My friend raised his hands and quickly followed with a disco double hip thrust, and two more stumbled backward, weapons dropping to their sides, eyes like goose eggs.

While my buddy's captivated females appeared to be losing their enthusiasm for mayhem, the rest of us, very subtly, began moving around in the plane. I was at the controls, readying for takeoff. Will was now casually moving backward toward the aircraft, still pretty much keeping the audience...dangling.

"Pray to the god of Jumping Bones," he cried, hands still out. "Worship the goddess of slapping bellies!"

Another hip thrust weakened the last of the resistant. Several women were on their knees now, the anticipation of belly slapping and jumping bones outweighing any sort of immediate umbrage.

A final hip thrust cost another woman her balance, and the ones left were swaying like saplings in the wind, eyes misty and wanting...weapons at their sides. Then, the next thing they knew, Will was scrambling for the Cessna and leaping onto a pontoon, then hanging on to a wing strut, and I was twisting the ignition switch. The engine fired, I eased the throttle in, and a few seconds later, we were streaking down the narrow channel into the misty darkness to the wail of wanting voices.

In moments, I had us on the main river and Will was being pulled aboard. I was checking gauges for a takeoff and my friend was throwing on some clothes.

Travis, who was riding copilot, turned around and looked back at Will, then spoke in that gruff voice of his. "I'm probably not ever gonna be able to look at you quite the same after that. But it was one of the more remarkable things I have witnessed in my life, and I've seen a few." He paused and smiled. "As a barroom story, it's certainly near the top of those worth telling."

That was probably as close as Travis ever got to a compliment. Will grinned and took it gladly.

"Let us ride into the night," cried Cody. "And may we all enjoy 'the horizontal mambo' sometime soon!"

"Here's to the four-legged tremble!" I yelled with a smile.

At that moment, Eddie, who was slumped against Cody in the back, awoke fully with a groan. His eye gradually cleared as he rubbed his chin. He looked at Cody and cocked his head. "Don't I know you, dude?"

"Yes, you do," replied his friend with a smile. "Indeed you do."

Behind us, on a small knoll at the edge of the moonlit water, stood a sorely disappointed, lustful group of ladies. No itches scratched. And Elvis had left the auditorium.

Dawn found us tying up our Cessna at the ramp of the Caracas airport FBO. We were all dog-tired, but God, it had been a good night — another one of those outrageous situations that would have to be told after the serious consumption of alcohol or no one would believe it.

We returned to the hotel and I put Eddie on the couch in the room Will and I shared, while my buddy took a much-needed shower. There wasn't too much conversation. It had been a long day and everyone was exhausted. But there seemed to be the slightest start of a recovery for Eddie. Earlier, while in the plane, he had looked at Travis and quietly said, "I think I know you too." He paused and muttered, "A coral wall..."

Travis reached back and patted him on the cheek. "Yeah, something like that, ol' buddy." Our big friend smiled — a thing he didn't do that often. "Welcome home, *amigo*," he said quietly. "Welcome home..."

Oorah...

The following day was consumed by meetings with the authorities — letting them know that Eddie had been found, and offering some assurances that no Indians or horses were actually killed in the process of making that movie.

In the short time we had been in Venezuela we had crashed an aircraft in a hurricane, were separated into bizarre circumstances, peripherally involved with a possible diamond theft, directly accused of participating in a bank robbery and the following unsanctioned distribution of stolen government money in Caracas, suspected of violating Venezuela's antiquities act with ancient artifacts, and possibly involved in the disappearance of three Smithsonian Institution employees (and a government helicopter), and then there was the recent rumor of us possibly participating in the disruption of an Amazon Indian village.

We were literally shown to the door of the country and asked to leave...and not come back.

We were quite okay with that. We loaded Cody's 310 and my 182 and bid Venezuela good-bye. We had taken it to the limit — hell, way past the limit — one more time...

CHAPTER SIXTEEN

Our return to civilization was most welcomed by all. Well, almost all. When the director of the Smithsonian heard that he had lost another three men and his organization might be implicated in the loss of a couple of Venezuelan military aircraft, he balanced on the edge of apoplexy.

Still, it wasn't much of a victory for us. We had lost the enigmatic crystal skull, and all the possible knowledge or abilities it might have contained. There was a satisfaction in having discovered it, and certainly for a few of us — Will, Rinco, and myself — the unique experience of the insightful, purely extraordinary connection it offered. But it was gone, buried in thousands of feet of water off the coast of Venezuela. Probably...

You win some. You lose some.

Regardless, it had been another remarkable adventure — a voyage of spirit and imagination, and well worth all the challenges for the stories we could tell.

After clearing Customs, storing the aircraft in our hangar, and dividing up our gear, we wished each other the best for a while. The kids returned to their place on Summerland. I brought Eddie home with me. At this point, he seemed to be identifying with me the most.

We stumbled into my house on Big Pine. I spent some time with my dog, then my friend, and I slept for the better part of a day. Over the next few days, Eddie definitely began coming back but it was a slow process. I was disappointed that we had returned without the crystal skull, but there was something about that entire affair...the yin and yang of high adventure. The whole damn thing was like dating a redhead on smack — it was exciting but you never knew when the shoe was going to drop. I was ready for a break. At least, that's what I wanted.

But the gods are the gods, mon. Sometimes good, sometimes surprising, sometimes terrible...

We'd been home well over a week and Eddie was showing

excellent signs of recovery. He recognized all of us now and was managing for himself back at his home (with us checking in on him), and while he wasn't quite ready to go back to work, things seemed to be balancing out for all of us. Then an ugly coincidence tumbled out of nowhere. It was a horrible reckoning that changed our plans. And our world.

Our buddy, Rinco, was also just settling into some peace and quiet. He was picking up some supplies at a local grocery store when one of Chakan's people recognized him. The guy was the only person who had escaped our recent Lower Keys attack, other than his boss. Chakan wasn't sure how far the hand of retribution extended, so he had left town — headed back to his fortress home in the Exumas for a while. But after about a week, he got bored and returned to South Florida.

Chakan's man had no place in particular to run after the compound gunfight, so he just hunkered down in Key West, pretty much lying low. He was buying wine at a store when he recognized Rinco. His eyes narrowed and he slid back around the aisle, out of sight.

When Rinco Rodriguez left the grocery store, the fellow discreetly followed him back to his small rental house on Southard Street. As Rinco parked his car and brought his groceries inside, the man smiled. It wasn't pretty. *Chakan would pay him well for this. Revenge was not just a required institution with the big Jamaican. It was a form of entertainment.* A half-hour later, he was on the phone with his boss man in Miami. "Ya, ya, mon, it was him — one of the *blancs* who destroyed the compound..."

Chakan listened intently, his emerald-green eyes brightening with interest, his pale white hands suddenly clutching the phone tightly. "You be sure, mon..." he whispered harshly. "Don' make me come to you for naught." The threat was veiled but real. No one disappointed Chakan without consequence.

"Ya mon, ya mon, I be sure. Promise on my firstborn. It is him! He can lead us to the others... Then we can kill him."

Bad luck is like the bullet that drops you in combat. You seldom see it coming... I don't know who said that, but the son of a bitch was right.

Later that night, after dinner and a couple bottles of beer, Rinco went out to lock his car before bedtime. He never saw the man who hit him with the blackjack. They dragged him back inside his house and when he came around, he found himself painfully bound to a kitchen chair. When the red haze cleared a little, there was the big Jamaican — *Refrigerator Man* — the same milky skin, tight yellow afro, heavy lips, big white teeth like tombstones, and those empty emerald eyes absolutely brimming with the pleasure of hate. The heavy man leaned into him, almost face to face.

"Dis not gonna be pleasurable for you, *blanc*, no matter how it come," he hissed. "But if you give me what I want, I give you peace without too much pain."

Rinco looked up at the guy and matched his stare, then barked with a military cadence, "Captain Rinco Don Rodriguez. U.S. Marines. Service number two seven five, zero four, zero nine, nine, four."

Chakan visibly flinched at the harsh, unexpected response. He backed up slightly. "Have it your way, *blanc,* but you gonna tell me what I want in the end…"

He exhaled and nodded to the man holding the long knife next to him. The fellow moved in and cut a three-inch gash in Rinco's forearm. The soldier gasped slightly, then his face settled without emotion, eyes straight ahead.

"Let's start easy," growled the big Jamaican. "Tell me the names of your friends."

My buddy looked up at his captor, deadpan. "Captain Rinco Don Rodriguez. United States Marines. Service number two seven five, zero four, zero nine, nine, four."

They tortured Rinco Rodriguez for a half hour. That's a long time in hell for anyone, even a Marine. They wanted the names of his friends and how to find them. Finally, when he could stand no more, our friend surrendered and gave them names.

"Okay…okay…" Rinco groaned, sweat-soaked and blood-covered. I'll tell you…I'll tell you. The big guy's name is…Jack… Jack London." He exhaled hard. "His friend, blond hair…it's Pete… Pete O'Toole… I think."

Chakan stared at him, uncertain. "I think I hear that name before."

Rinco groaned and spit blood on the floor. "Yeah…he's pretty well known around here…"

For the next couple of minutes, he gasped and spit blood, and continued, slowly, painfully, letting them pull the other names from him. Mick Mantle, Johnny Unitas, Herb Hoover…and he gave them addresses for them as well — whatever came to mind. And at the end, when a thoroughly uncertain Chakan held a gun to his captor's head and asked him if he had any last words, Marine Captain Rinco Rodriguez — ravaged, bloody, and just this side of the other side — looked up. He offered a final smile and gasped, "Semper Fi… Oorah…"

Spirit took our friend's hand just before the gun went off…and in what seemed like only a moment, he was standing in the wheat field by his parents' house. The sun was brilliant and warm, and there was Custer, running at him, eyes bright, tongue lolling, barking joyously. Rinco Don Rodriguez smiled. He was home.

It was me who found him. I had stopped by the following afternoon while running errands in Key West, after I had left messages and heard nothing in return. It was out of character for my new buddy. I'd gladly pay just about anything to wipe that scene from my mind. Some people say that through pain there is growth. I don't believe that. Pain is just pain, and it sucks…

I called Travis and he met me there, at the house, then we called the police. Our team spent the evening with the police answering questions. We had sort of a love-hate relationship with the authorities. They knew we were the good guys, basically, but we were way too unconventional to make them happy.

There was little doubt who had done this. In fact, the police said their informants were already whispering about the drug lord, Chakan, being headed out of the country, back to his fortress in the Exumas. The man was originally from Jamaica and he had a history of crime from the very beginning — Negril Town gangs and trips into Haiti with low-level contraband, but he quickly graduated to drug running, and when the price was right, "disappearing" people. His extraordinary looks and ruthlessness moved him up in the ranks. As he slid into power and position, he had purchased a large home on a private bay near the center of Exuma Island, which is conveniently midway between Jamaica and South Florida. Chakan turned it into a fortress. He bought off a fair portion of the officials, including most of the police on the island. The word was, he was damned near untouchable when he reached those shores.

"I don't care if he's fled to hell," Travis hissed, his eyes on fire. "I'm coming for the son of a bitch! There's no place on God's green earth he can hide."

We were about to get seriously unconventional. Ugly unconventional. I could tell by the look on Travis's face when he saw what they had done to our friend.

Travis turned to us when we got outside. "I want this son of a bitch. I wanna kill this Chakan bastard with my hands," he growled. "I want to watch the life leave his eyes..." He glared at each of us and exhaled. "Suit up," he said. "Or don't, because this is gonna get ugly." He stared at us. "I'm gonna bury this man and everyone around him. I'm gonna burn him out of his island stronghold and grind him into the dirt with my heel."

It was Cody's turn then. He looked around at us, his blue eyes hard as marbles. "We'll take tomorrow to organize, then leave at dawn the following day. Bring your favorite weapons." Our friend paused. His eyes were burning now. "And let loose the dogs of war!"

I have to tell you, the transformation in my friends scared the shit out of me...and I was on their side. But the truth was, I felt the same way. This was an extraordinary man these bastards had taken — a fine American soldier and a person with a good heart, and his own plan for the world to make it a better place.

Yeah, Cody was right. *Let loose the dogs of war...*

When I told the kids, they were horrified but their anger overrode their fear. When I said they weren't going with us, that it was just too dangerous, my son looked at me and for the first time, I saw a different person. He was no longer a youngster, untried and green. He was a man burning with rage. There wasn't a drop of fear in his entire countenance, and Jing, standing next to him, was his exact mirror.

"Try and stop us," Tax growled. "Try and stop us! He was our friend too!" He stared at me. "I don't believe in any of those pansy-assed, bullshit quotes about understanding, forgiveness, and restraint. I want retribution. I want vengeance!" He let out a long breath, his eyes still boring holes into me. "I want blood."

The following morning, while I contacted the military offices for the Marines in Key West regarding our friend's funeral, Travis contacted the U.S. Marshals Office and the Drug Enforcement Authority (DEA) and called in a couple of favors. The retired head of the DEA had a son, a young Army officer at the time, who had served with distinction in Vietnam. But he had gotten his ass into a sling during the 1972 Easter Offensive, and he and the remaining men in his patrol would have "bought property" there that day if it wasn't for a certain helicopter pilot with more balls than brains — Captain Travis Christian.

Retired Colonel Robert Landman ("Old Landmine" as he was called, sometimes affectionately) took the call. An hour later, we had a complete dossier on Jean Shan Pachoute, who called himself Chakan.

The chatter was right — Chakan owned a fortress of sorts on the eastern coast of Exuma Island. He had become a fairly high-level drug smuggler (cocaine mostly) but had interests in gambling as well. He had some ownership in a casino in Port-au-Prince, and some street operations in South Florida — anything that would turn a dollar. The dog-fighting thing in the Keys wasn't big money. He was just slumming there, just keeping his Key West contacts fed for when he might need them.

Chakan was also a suspect in the murder of a DEA operative in South Florida but he was a hard man to put a finger on. Whenever things got sticky, he slipped back to his home base north of George Town in Exuma Island. It was an inconspicuous little island with a small tourist trade — basically a no man's land and a tough place for American authorities to operate. Because he owned many of the police there and could come and go with impunity. There weren't near enough authorities to cover that string of islands, and half of the constables would turn their back on a hatchet murder if the price was right.

That's where we were headed.

CHAPTER SEVENTEEN

The next day, we all waited at my place until late afternoon. Everyone, including Tax, Jing, and the hawk. There was no question, this was going to get ugly. We were going to come in quick, just after dusk. No Customs. Just do what we had to do and get out.

I hadn't wanted the kids in the middle of it. Neither had Will. He'd gone a couple of rounds with Jing the night before and lost, same as me. We just didn't own enough "credits" — we hadn't paid the dues as parents to have a say. In the end, they were adults, and both of them were valuable assets in a tight spot. They deserved the right to choose their pleasure or their poison. And Rinco had been their friend, too...

During that time, we studied the map and the information the DEA had supplied Travis. Will, ever the historian, also gave us a brief feel for the Exuma Islands, the most important being Exuma itself.

"The Exumas were first populated by the Lucayan Indians, who welcomed the Spanish conquistadores with open arms in the 16th century, and were promptly enslaved, then completely annihilated by the 17th century," he explained. "Same old story... Later, the Exumas were settled in the early 1780s by American Loyalists fleeing the Revolutionary War. They brought with them the concept of the cotton plantation economy, which required lots of...'help.' But the sandy soil gave out and the cotton industry died, leaving a lot of African slaves, who soon became free in the 1800s. This changed the complexion of the Exumas forever." Will drew a breath. "The capital city is George Town. John Rolle, an early Loyalist settler, played a major role in the island's future, bestowing all his significant land holdings to his slaves when he died. When the land gave out, the Exumas lost significance until the 1900s, when a fledgling tourist industry began."

He paused. "The Exumas Islands do draw some tourists but they have never been a major tourist place — too flat and hot, not as close as the Bahamas, and not offering anything unique, like the mountains of Jamaica. But they're perfect for 'businessmen' like Chakan. A safe place for a person with money, regardless of who you are, and not much law enforcement to bother you. This is what we're up against. Whatever we're going to do, it has to be surgical and quick, before the authorities figure out what's happening and set up roadblocks."

"Once we find him, it'll be quick," growled Travis from a stool at the kitchen bar. "Quicker than he deserves…"

Looking at a map, Will explained that there was really only one main road on the island, which ran north to south on the east side. Most all the settlements and tourist resorts split off on smaller roads from that. Chakan's small fortress was located on a remote point just south of the largely undeveloped Flamingo Bay. He even had a small, personal airstrip about a half mile from the house. But we were using my Cessna 182 and planned to land in the bay adjacent to the home. If I could get us in quietly enough. A long glide from maybe an altitude of five thousand feet, and a quiet, dead-stick landing would put us in Chakan's lap without much more than the sound of the wind under the wings.

The less than two-hour flight down into Exuma Island was smooth and easy, almost no weather to contend with. Once again, I had decided to leave Shadow with my attractive neighbor, who had the female Rottweiler my boy liked so much. I didn't know what to expect on this trip, and I still recalled, vividly, my recent loss of him in the jungle. I couldn't deal with that again. Jing, however, wouldn't be parted from Cielo. No one argued. We'd seen that arrangement pay off more than once.

Just before takeoff, I had duct-taped over my plane's identification numbers. No point giving anyone a positive ID on us.

The DEA's man on Exuma Island was certain that Chakan was hiding there again in his palatial home. No neighbors for a quarter-mile in any direction. That worked for him, but it also worked for us. That meant no one paying attention to our "soft approach."

Five miles out, I climbed a little higher. The last of the sun was slipping into the horizon and the shadows were growing long. The sky had lost its battle with the night and everything was darkening.

I looked at the team and muttered, "Here we go."

"For Captain Rinco Rodriguez," growled Cody.

"Oorah!" muttered Travis adamantly.

"Oorah!" we all replied.

I turned off the ignition, pushed the nose down slightly, and dropped about twenty-five percent of my flaps. The lady at my hands responded in a silent, controlled fall — a lot like a hawk that had chosen its target.

Of the two guards that Chakan had walking the upper decks of the house, one had taken this moment to use the restroom and the other was enjoying a smoke on the far side of the building, facing the road. We came in on the bay, at their backs, silent as death. I drifted down in total silence, prop windmilling, touching the dark water about three hundred yards from the house, the plane somewhat protected by an old rock jetty that extended out a hundred yards or so and groups of palms along the shore. We tied up there and before we had all our gear readied, the shadows of night were claiming the bay.

We checked our weapons. Travis had a semi-automatic riot shotgun and his "dogleg 45" pistol. Cody carried his trusty Thompson machine gun with a circular magazine and a silenced 9mm. Both Will and I carried short-barreled 20-gauge shotguns and .380 pistols at our shoulders. Tax had chosen a 12-gauge shotgun and Jing was carrying a .38 revolver at her waist. But she also had that perpetually dangerous weapon in the air above her — Cielo.

Travis glanced around at us. "Time to get on with this," he said, staring at us all. "Tonight you are at war. There is no mercy or kindness here. There is no negotiation. Tonight is about revenge. Tonight is about killing rats..."

Travis slipped on a pair of night goggles and took the lead. The rest of us stumbled quietly behind him. We moved away, quiet as wraiths, working our way around the curved shoreline and the ever-present mangroves. The mosquitoes buzzed around us hungrily, our repellent barely discouraging them.

It wasn't long before we could hear the voices of the guards on the ground and the walkways of the huge home. None of them seemed all that attentive.

The truth was, who in their right minds would attack a major Caribbean drug lord on his home turf, in a place where he owned the police?

The first serious obstacle was an eight-foot-tall chain-link fence. But thanks to the DEA photographs from Travis's friends, it wasn't unexpected. Our bolt cutters put us through while the two men who patrolled the interior perimeter were on the opposite side of the compound.

The house was a typical "rich" Caribbean structure — concrete block covered with stucco and coral rock on the exterior walls, with a Spanish barrel tile roof. But it was huge — over four thousand square feet. There was a tower-like structure at one end and walkways that ran around the upper exterior of the place, along with two cars and a pickup parked under the open front deck. And there were a couple of outbuildings — storage, etc.

We were crouching in the darkness at the periphery of the fence, among a handful of fifty-gallon drums, as the two grounds guards began to make their way toward us.

"Com'on, boys," grated Cody. "Come on…"

The guards had come around the exterior and were now moving parallel to us, carrying on a heated conversation. We had been told that all of Chakan's people were Haitian. He didn't trust anyone else. Listening to them talk as they came along, I was reminded how distinctly different the accents/vernacular of the blacks in the Bahamas and Jamaica are from Haiti. The Jamaican and Bahamian Africans had a fairly pleasant accent compared to the Haitian dialect, which was heavy and almost guttural, and now grated against my ears.

Ultimately, it didn't matter for these two. Cody, crouching in the shadows, shot them both with his silenced pistol. No mercy, no honor, no regret. Tonight we were killing rats. Tonight would be retribution and revenge, damned sure as pure a part of man as his mercy and kindness, and every bit as necessary to his composition — and for the survival of the species.

Most people in this "kind new world" didn't like to admit it, but the fear of reprisal and the power of the sword were the very cornerstones of civilized society. They're what has kept this species relatively balanced since the first caveman was pushed off a cliff for stealing the clan's food. You remove them and what you've got is people running wild in the streets, burning and looting.

There didn't seem to be any other guards on the exterior grounds but I could hear voices above us from the interior of the huge home. The size of the house was an intimidating challenge and the unknown number of assailants made it worse. Some of the help in the place may have been bad guys as well. I asked Travis about that.

"Kill 'em all," he growled. "And let God sort it out."

Travis was a tough man but I had never seen him like this. He was terrifying. I never realized how much he'd taken to Rinco. Looking back, I think he saw a younger version of himself in Rinco and our friend's tragic death had struck a deep chord within him.

Travis calmed for a moment and looked at me. "You see people who don't look like antagonists, make your own call. But you get one of us killed and I'm gonna shoot you."

After that little "no-win" statement, I decided that maybe having God sort it out was the best thing.

We shot up all the resistance on the outside and headed inside. There were a couple of more in-house guards who God was quickly sorting. One had hidden around a corner near the upper balcony above the huge living room, and was proving difficult to get to. He had the advantage of high ground. I looked at Jing and the hawk on her arm. She nodded, then turned to Cielo and spoke to him in that strange, guttural language. Then she moved her arm and showed him, pointing... I've seen some amazing things in my life, but those two, that girl and that damned winged creature, are still right near the top. It was like a Las Vegas act — a very deadly act.

The hawk spread those huge wings and made a wide circle to the tall, domed ceiling, just above the antagonist now. Travis drew the man out with a couple of rounds. That was all Cielo needed. He half folded his wings and dropped in a short curve. The fellow was concentrating on us (who would expect to be set upon by an attack hawk, really...). The bird hit him with a glancing blow of those terrible talons, which got all his attention. He made the mistake of stumbling out of the hallway to the banister, where Travis took him out.

All the help had locked themselves in the pantry. I took a chance, shot the lock, and went in. There was nobody dangerous there — a couple of hookers, a chef, and some kitchen people. I closed the door so they didn't get "sorted out."

I could hear shooting in various parts of the house. I hoped to God our people were winning.

Inside of ten minutes, it got quiet, and to my great relief, Jing and Tax came down from upstairs, Jing's hawk on her arm, another hooker on Tax's arm. There was blood running down his shoulder but he didn't look like he was critical.

Travis went over to the hooker. Just seeing Travis this angry was enough to loosen my bladder. He had the same effect on the hooker, who peed her pants while he questioned her.

The good news was, we owned the place. The bad news was, one of the hookers got a phone call from Chakan as we were invading. He been running south, toward George Town, just to get out of Dodge, but when he heard how bad things had gone, he turned around and was heading for his private field about five miles away.

If he got to a fast twin there, he'd be gone for good. He'd bury himself in Haiti for a while, then maybe end up in Central or South America.

Travis turned to me. "Run! Head for your plane and get it in the air. Drop it in on the road out front here and pick me up. We gotta get Chakan before he gets to that airfield!"

Adrenaline being what it is, I might have broken a record on the three-hundred-yard dash. I threw myself into the cockpit and had the prop turning in thirty seconds. Whirling the plane around on the water, I shot out and lifted off as soon as the airspeed indicator hit the right numbers. In moments, I had brought the bird around, my port wing almost dragging the water, and skipped across the surface to the road in front of the mansion. Travis was waiting, waving me down. He never even let the plane stop, he just ran alongside, then grabbed the wing strut, threw himself up onto the pontoon and ripped open the door. A moment later, he was pulling himself into the seat next to me.

"What are you waiting for?" he yelled. "Get this damned thing in the air!"

There was, as usual, some good news and some bad news here. The good news was, we were going to make it to the airfield in about four minutes. The bad news was, Chakan was already there, sitting in the passenger's seat while his pilot cranked the twin bird's engines. In just seconds they were rolling down to the threshold and the pilot was turning the plane around for takeoff. Once he had that bird in the air, the game was over. There was absolutely no catching them with my plane.

As we reached the field, the Haitian's plane was running down the strip, about thirty seconds from getting enough wind under that bird for takeoff.

"Get down next to him," Travis screamed over the engine and the wind, bringing up his pump shotgun.

I slipped down, throttle to the wall, making up a few seconds in my drop over the airfield runway. Our one advantage was that neither Chakan nor the pilot had seen us coming at them like a hawk. I pushed the throttle to the wall again, and suddenly, for just a few seconds, we were running next to the twin, just slightly higher — my high starboard wing above the low port wing of the other plane. It was like a bloody circus act! But with that fast twin, this was a limited-time offer.

At that moment, three things happened: First, Chakan and his pilot suddenly saw us, not twenty feet over and to the side of them. Second, Travis knocked out the passenger's window of my bird with the butt of his shotgun. And third, the big Haitian's green eyes got larger as Travis aimed his gun and fired, point-blank at the cockpit, until it clicked.

Chakan wasn't killed right away but his pilot was, which, needless to say, was not good for the Haitian. When the pilot's brain quit working (due to buckshot poisoning) the small twin veered, then twisted. I quickly turned away and rose out, avoiding contact (and multiple funerals for the good guys), as the twin below turned and dug a wing into the ground. It flipped, then rolled, crushing a wing and crumpling, then skidding to a stop upside down. Almost immediately smoke billowed out of the cockpit.

I had our plane down on the ground a minute later and we pulled up behind the burning aircraft. Travis got out and walked over to it, not particularly in a hurry. He bent down by the passenger's side window, which was gone now. A very badly wounded Chakan lolled over and looked up at him, those huge green eyes filled with pain and terror. The smell of gas was all-

GODS, GUNS, AND MONEY ON THE ROAD TO KEY WEST

pervading. The whole thing was going to go up in seconds. Still, Travis squatted down next to the trapped man and stared at him.

"Save me," begged the Haitian. "The plane, the fire…I don't want to die like this. Please…"

"You killed a good man," growled Travis. "A really good man, and you made him die hard." He eased out a sigh. "Sometimes in life you get exactly what you deserve." My friend exhaled. "I'll probably see you in Hell, and if I do, I'm gonna kill you again, just because."

The flames were spreading through the aircraft, only seconds away from the gas tanks. Travis stood and started to turn away, then he sighed angrily and tossed his pistol to the trapped man.

"That's the best deal you're gonna get today," he hissed. "And you're fresh out of tomorrows." Then he walked away.

The shot came five seconds before the plane exploded in flames.

We could hear the sirens in the background. It was about to get sticky in lots of ways. Travis and I jumped back into my Cessna and headed back to our team at Chakan's mansion. We loaded up at the seawall and moments later, I had us climbing out of "paradise lost."

EPILOGUE

The return home was bittersweet. Yes, we had avenged our friend and probably put a small dent in the illicit businesses of South Florida, but we had still lost a friend. In the short time I had known Rinco Rodriguez, he had made a profound impression on me, and I knew it was the same with the others. He was one of those extraordinary souls that we are, on occasion, permitted to touch and to be touched by. Each and every one of us felt the same way.

Most uniquely, Rinco had found purpose in life — an incredibly valuable commodity that most of us seek but never find. He was a hard and capable soul when he had to be, but there was a vein of kindness and compassion that ran deeply through him and he had found a way to exercise that. And in the process, Rinco had changed the world.

We couldn't have known then, but Rinco Rodriguez, aka Animal Man, was not to be easily forgotten — not by a long shot. In fact, he was about to become moderately famous. From his integrity and courage, and his compassion toward animals, would be born a whole new generation of human beings in the service of kindness toward lesser creatures. *Animal Men and Women.*

The local Marines contingent in Key West gave our friend a full honors funeral. The *Key West Citizen* made him "Citizen of the Week" posthumously, telling the remarkable story of his "outside-the-box" dedication and courage for man's animal companions. A surprising number of people stepped forward to tell their stories about him and how he helped desperate creatures. I loved the quote that they took from Rinco's notes and added to the article:

You too can be an Animal Man, or Woman, any time you see a domestic creature being abused or mistreated. All it takes is an outrage to pain and suffering, and a pair of cajones — real or imagined.

You don't have to do this alone — get a couple of friends with the same ideology and guts to become Animal Men (or women) with you. When you discover a "situation" don't be afraid to confront!

Accept it! Deal with it! Get creative! Remember, people who mistreat animals are generally laggards and cowards. Confront and challenge together, as a team, and if that doesn't work, act! A baseball bat and a car windshield is a good way to get attention. Use your imagination and your courage. It's how you change the world. Anyone can be an Animal Man!

Sometimes, something just strikes a chord in the hearts of good men and women...a combination of empathy, admiration, and grit. Within two weeks after Rinco's death, there were two new Animal Men in Key West, one taking messages at the same Sloppy Joe's blackboard and one at the Green Parrot poolroom blackboard.

Inside of six weeks, there were three Animal Men in Miami and Homestead. Several of the South Florida newspapers picked up on this unique "public service idea." In another two months, there were Animal Men in Tampa, Saint Petersburg, and Jacksonville. Oddly enough, three of the more amicable motorcycle gangs in Florida had joined the wave. Their reluctance to take any shit from anyone made them rather refreshing Animal Men.

Newspapers started picking up on this new movement of courage and kindness, and the beneficial, somewhat unsanctioned power of men and women. Yes...Animal Women as well! (Never anger a woman when dealing with a helpless creature — you're just asking for trouble.)

Six months later, the concept had spread across the southern United States — New Orleans; Jackson, Mississippi; Montgomery, Alabama; and Nashville, Tennessee, to name a few — and those who had a penchant for animal cruelty or an indifference to the health and well-being of lesser creatures were put on notice. Hell, they were being outright persecuted.

Within one year, the concept had gone from the vision of a single man to a fresh new ideology and a new way of looking at our furred companions and ourselves. And more importantly, it had changed the lives of thousands of helpless creatures.

Oorah!

***THIS BOOK IS DEDICATED TO ANIMAL MEN AND
WOMEN EVERYWHERE***

*All it takes is an outrage to pain and suffering, and a pair
of cajones — real or imagined.*

— Rinco Rodriguez

I hope you have enjoyed this novel. If you would like to be added to my mailing list (to stay apprised of new novels and to receive bimonthly updates and my newspaper columns), email me at: reisig@ipa.net

—*Michael Reisig*

And…be sure to read the rest of
Michael Reisig's best-selling

ROAD TO KEY WEST SERIES

THE ROAD TO KEY WEST

The Road to Key West is an adventurous, humorous sojourn that cavorts its way through the 1970s Caribbean, from Key West and the Bahamas to Cuba and Central America—a Caribbean brew of part-time pirates, heartless larcenists, wild women, Voodoo bokors, drug smugglers, and a wacky Jamaican soothsayer.

Kindle Book only $3.99
To Preview or Purchase this book on amazon.com, use this link:
http://www.amazon.com/dp/B004RPMYF8

BACK ON THE ROAD TO KEY WEST
The Golden Scepter — Book II

An ancient map and a lost pirate treasure, a larcenous Bahamian scoundrel with his gang of cutthroats, a wild and crazy journey into South America in search of a magical antediluvian device, and perilous, hilarious encounters with outlandish villains and zany friends will keep you locked to your seat and giggling maniacally.

Kindle Book only $3.99
To Preview or Purchase this book on amazon.com, use this link:
http://www.amazon.com/dp/B00FC9D94I

ALONG THE ROAD TO KEY WEST
The Truthmaker — Book III

Fast-paced humor and adventure with wacky pilots, quirky con men, mad villains, bold women, and a gadget to die for. Florida Keys adventurers Kansas Stamps and Will Bell find their lives turned upside down when they discover a truth device hidden in the temple of an ancient civilization. Enthralled by the virtue of personally dispensing truth and justice with this unique tool, they soon discover everyone wants what they have—from the government to the Vatican.

Kindle Book only $3.99
To Preview or Purchase this book on amazon.com, use this link:
http://www.amazon.com/dp/B00G5B3HEY

SOMEWHERE ON THE ROAD TO KEY WEST
The Emerald Cave — Book IV

The captivating diary of an amateur archaeologist sends our intrepid explorers on a journey into the heart of the Panamanian jungle in search of *la cueva de Esmeralda* (the Emerald Cave), and a lost Spanish treasure. But local brigand Tu Phat Shong and his gang of cutthroats are searching for the same treasure. If that wasn't enough, one of the Caribbean's nastiest drug lords has a score to settle with our reluctant heroes.

Kindle Book only $3.99
To Preview or Purchase this book on amazon.com, use this link:
http://www.amazon.com/dp/B00NOABMKA

DOWN THE ROAD TO KEY WEST
Pancho Villa's Gold — Book V

If you're looking for clever fun with zany characters, a and electric high adventure, this one's for you! Reisig's newest offering is guaranteed to keep you locked to your seat and slapping at the pages, while burbling up a giggle or two. In the fifth book of this series, our reluctant Caribbean heroes find themselves competing for the affections of a beautiful antiquities dealer and searching for the lost treasure of Mexico's most renowned desperado.

Kindle Book only $3.99
To Preview or Purchase this book on amazon.com, use this link:
http://www.amazon.com/dp/B01EPI6XY4

BEYOND THE ROAD TO KEY WEST
Mayan Gold — Book VI

First, the reader is drawn back over 400 years, to the magnificent Mayan empire — to the intrigue of powerful rulers, Spanish invasion, and an adventure/love story that survives the challenge of time. Moving forward several centuries, Kansas and Will stumble upon a collection of ancient writings, and the tale of a treasure that was cached by the great Mayan ruler, Nachán Can...

Kindle book only 3.99
To Preview or Purchase this book on amazon.com, use this link:
http://www.amazon.com/dp/B01M293NDP

A FAR ROAD TO KEY WEST
Emeralds and Lies — Book VII

The "Hole in the Coral Wall Gang" return to the Guatemalan jungle to retrieve the remainder of a Mayan king's incredible treasure, but in the process they find themselves engaged in a grassroots revolution, pursued by a vengeful colonel in the Guatemalan military, and immersed in the intrigue of a World War Two Nazi treasure. Then, there's the beautiful sister of a revolutionary, the golden Swiss francs, and the greatest challenge of all — *Granja Penal de Pavón* — the most terrifying prison in all of Central America.

To Preview or Purchase this book on amazon.com, use this link:
http://www.amazon.com/dp/B072VRR2VY

THE WILD ROAD TO KEY WEST
The Cave of The Stars —- Book VIII

Once again, the Hole in the Coral Wall Gang is wrapped in a wild adventure. Diamonds and emeralds, a lost city infused by a treasure and an ancient race, a secret cave with a timeless message, ruthless bandits, jungle Indians, and nefarious cowboys are all part of this non-stop roller coaster ride.

Did I mention the gang's new guide, Arturio — a Venezuelan outback opportunist who has a mild obsession with Russian Roulette? Or Passi, the lustful jungle witch who just can't make up her mind?

To Preview or Purchase this book on amazon.com, use this link::
www.amazon.com/dp/B078FMD5TZ

A PIRATE'S ROAD TO KEY WEST
Lafitte's Gold Book — Book IX

In the ninth novel of his best-selling "Road To Key West" series, Michael Reisig once again locks his readers into a careening odyssey of hidden fortunes, mercurial romance, conscienceless villains, and bizarre friends.

From Caracas to New Orleans, into the dark fringes of Haiti, down through the Windward Islands, then back into the Florida Keys, Kansas Stamps, Will Bell, and the Hole in the Coral Wall Gang chase a stolen Pre-Columbian treasure. Then there's the Voodoo-practicing drug boss, a vengeful Colombian don, and a highly artful assassin. Before you can catch your breath, it all rolls together into a turbulent Key West Fantasy Fest finale.

To Preview or Purchase this book on amazon.com, use this link:
https://www.amazon.com/PIRATES-ROAD-KEY-
WEST/dp/0999091476

THE LOST ROAD TO KEY WEST
The Pharaoh's Gold — Book X

Take a wild journey, from ancient Egyptian explorations to modern-day discoveries in the walls of the mystical Grand Canyon. It's history and mythology mixed with hard-hitting real time adventure. Did I mention, the osprey, and the "hit girls" and the gold?

To Preview or Purchase this book on amazon.com, use this link:
https://amzn.to/2z2oo8w

THE INCREDIBLE KEY WEST-CARIBBEAN RACE

Kansas stamps and Will Bell are back in an absolutely roaring Caribbean adventure that may be the most unique of Reisig's tales to date.

After a night of Key West carousing, the boys find themselves entangled in a contest of sorts — a race, or perhaps more correctly, a series of challenges that carry them across the Caribbean and into Central and South America. (We're talking about villainous villains, wild Texan promoters, hit men, biker gangs, beautiful crazy women, mad Colombian dons, moonlit voodoo ceremonies, sailing races and hurricanes, and an island with creatures that would keep your nightmares awake.)

Kindle Book only $2.99
To Preview or Purchase this book on amazon.com, use this link:
https://www.amazon.com/Incredible-Key-West-Caribbean-Race/dp/057870207X

THE TRUE TALES OF THE ROAD TO KEY WEST

These tales will make you smile with wonder, remind you of the importance of loyalty and love in life, and make you laugh your ass off. I have taken my experiences, encounters, and adventures, and blended them into and around the highlights of my eight "Road To Key West" novels. Included in the package are a number of memory-jarring photos and terrific quotes, to create a humorous, insightful, walk down memory lane for new and seasoned readers.

If you haven't read any of "The Road To Key West" novels, this is the perfect place to begin. If you've read them all, you'll love these engaging, sometimes laugh-out-loud recollections.

Kindle Book only $2.99
To Preview or Purchase this book on amazon.com, use this link:
https://www.amazon.com/True-Tales-Road-Key-West/dp/0999091468

Also, be sure to read...

CARIBBEAN GOLD
THE TREASURE OF TORTUGA

In 1668, Englishman Trevor Holte and the audacious freebooter Clevin Greymore sail from the Port of London for the West Indies. They set out in search of adventure and wealth, but the challenges they encounter are beyond their wildest dreams—the brutal Spanish, ruthless buccaneers, a pirate king, the lure of Havana, and the women, as fierce in their desires as Caribbean storms. And then, there was the gold—wealth beyond imagination. But some treasures outlive the men who bury them...

Kindle Book only $3.99
To Preview or Purchase this book on amazon.com, use this link:
http://www.amazon.com/dp/B00S8SR0WW

CARIBBEAN GOLD
THE TREASURE OF TIME

In the spring of 1980, three adventurers set out from Key West in search of a lost treasure on the Isle of Tortuga, off the coast of Haiti. Equipped with an ancient parchment and a handful of clues, they embark on a journey that carries them back across time, challenging their courage and their imaginations, presenting them with remarkable allies and pitting them against an amalgam of unrelenting enemies. In the process, they uncover far more than a treasure. They discover the power of friendship and faith, the unflagging capacity of spirit, and come to realize that some things are forever...

Kindle Book only $3.99
To Preview or Purchase this book on amazon.com, use this link:
http://www.amazon.com/dp/B00S8SR0WW

CARIBBEAN GOLD
THE TREASURE OF MARGARITA

The Treasure of Margarita spans three centuries of high adventure. Beginning in 1692, in the pirate stronghold of Port Royal, it carries the reader across the Southern Hemisphere in a collage of rip-roaring escapades. Then it soars forward five generations, into modern-day intrigue and romance in Key West and the Caribbean.

A staggering fortune of Spanish black pearls and a 300-year-old letter with a handful of clues set the course that Travis Christian and William Cody embark upon. But it's not an easy sail. Seasoned with remarkable women and bizarre villains, the adventure ricochets from one precarious situation to the next.

Kindle Book only $3.99
To Preview or Purchase this book on amazon.com, use this link:
http://www.amazon.com/dp/B00X1E2X2K

Made in the USA
Monee, IL
04 May 2021

67696122R00105